Joseph Henry Pearce

Tales of the Masque

Joseph Henry Pearce

Tales of the Masque

ISBN/EAN: 9783337082215

Printed in Europe, USA, Canada, Australia, Japan

Cover: Foto ©Andreas Hilbeck / pixelio.de

More available books at **www.hansebooks.com**

TALES OF THE MASQUE.

BY

J. H. PEARCE,

AUTHOR OF "JACO TRELOAR," ETC.

LONDON:

LAWRENCE AND BULLEN,

18, HENRIETTA ST., COVENT GARDEN.

1894.

LONDON :
PRINTED BY WOODFALL AND KINDER,
70 TO 76, LONG ACRE, W.C.

CONTENTS.

THE LITTLE CROW OF PARADISE.

B

THE LITTLE CROW OF PARADISE.

On the walls of heaven there dwells a little black crow: and this is the tale of how his happiness was attained.

Once a year, as we know, the robin goes to hell, bearing a drop of water in its beak. The water is for some poor soul in torment whom the robin loves in spite of his sins: the power to take the journey and to return from it unscathed, having been granted by Christ to the robin for its kindness to Him when He hung upon the cross.

But to no other bird is this grace

extended; and into their songs there creeps, in consequence, a strangely sorrowful note.

Now the crow at the crucifixion—he has been the Devil's bird always—did nothing but cry mockingly, *Ha ! ha! ha!* And though he could speak then as well as you or I—the Devil having granted him the gift of speech—ever since that day when he mocked the Saviour he has been reduced to a hoarse and melancholy *caw.*

But not all the crows have a cinder for a heart : here and there one has a heart indeed.

And one day such an one loved a man, and loved him faithfully. But the man was so steeped in sins that his soul, when it went to judgment, was as black as the feathers of its one sole friend : and no other portion could be granted to it but hell.

And when the crow heard, swaying in his nest among the elms, that the friend who had fed and fondled him was in torment—was in the awful Pit of the Great Thirst, with the lidless eyes of Satan fixed unsleepingly upon him—ah, *then* the crow's heart was humanised by sorrow ; and he grieved for his friend as a woman might have grieved.

"Will you take him a drop of water ?" said the crow to the robin.

"He has done nothing to deserve it," said the robin. "He must thirst."

"Then I will take him a drop of water myself," said the crow.

So he went to the spring among the elm-trees, where the water bubbled coolingly, and with a drop of water in his beak he flew down the world to hell.

As he dipped below the horizon into

the dreary world of darkness he could hear, floating up from the fathomless pit beneath him, the lamentable moaning and sighing of the Lost: and the crow's heart swelled with pity as he listened. That far-off world, with its nest among the elm-trees, he would give up gladly, if he might only ease his friend!

Down the vast black depths the crow sank heavily: down, and ever down, unrestingly downwards; down—down—down—till at last he was in hell.

In the black Pit of Thirst his friend moaned helplessly: his throat and lips parched into horrible blackness, and the sharp brine running through his veins instead of blood.

"Water! Give me water!" he gasped to the crow.

The crow sank down and, alighting on his shoulder, poured the cherished drop of water between the black, parched lips.

" A hundred years of agony have rolled away from me ! " gasped the man. " Now caw to me once, that I may remember the woodlands . . . ."

" *Caw !* " cried the little black crow : " *Caw ! caw !* "

But at that moment the Ancient One— who is of stone and without a heart— thrust his huge claws forward : and the crow was in his palm !

Then God, who seeth all things, was moved to compassion : and, as His thought became a deed, Satan's huge claws opened and up flew the little crow straight to Paradise ; alighting, singed and panting, on the vast gold walls.

Except the dove, no bird has ever entered heaven. The crow might not be admitted to the shining streets of pearl, but within sight of heaven he should dwell for ever, said the Merciful One. And on the great gold walls, against which the water of life ripples musically, the Little Crow of Paradise still builds his nest.

A VOYAGE TO THE GOLDEN· LAND.

A VOYAGE TO THE GOLDEN LAND.

" How do'ee knaw they islands ovver there are the wans they mayned ? " asked the Softie, incredulously.

" Warn't I up Trebedhow* weth them, an' heerd what they said ? They towld me to shaw them they owld burrows† up 'pon cleff, an' when I shawed them to them they gov' me this here sexpence ! " And Jimmy, diving into his trousers'-pocket, displayed the cherished bit of silver on his remarkably dirty palm.

" Iss ; but what about heaven bein' out

* The place of graves.   † Barrows.

there to Scilly ?*   I want to knaw 'zackly what they said about that."

"Well, wan o' the genelmen, he said, says he, 'twar all'ys the way o' some folks (I cudn catch their names) to be buried as close as they cud git to the sunset— that there colour up in the sky when the sun do go down.   An' he said how they folks buried up Trebedhow was buried 'pon the cleffs, so close to the say as they cud git, so's they'd have onnly a li'l way to go when they was sperrits : onnly 'cross to the islands out past the Wolf."†

"Iss ?" said Zeke, drawing a deep breath, and his clouded eyes beginning to brighten a little.

"He said the Wolf out there was where

---

* The old British name for the Scilly Islands was Sulléh—the rocks consecrated to the sun.

† An isolated rock between the Land's End and the Scilly Islands.

a gayte black dog lived ; 'a used to ayte up the ghostes, ef 'a cud catch them——"

" Doan't ! " cried Zeke. " I doan't like to hear that ! "

" But I'm sure 'bout Scilly, Zeke : sartin sure ! " And Jimmy, who was lying on the cliff-top on his stomach, wriggled forward with a look of intense conviction on his face. " I'm sartin sure, 'cos I axed the genelman ! ' Es heaven ovver there, sir ; ovver to Scilly, sir ? ' I axed un. An' 'a laughed rayle plaised, weth 'es haands in 'es pockets, an' 'es gayte gowld watch-chain shinin' some lovely. ' So they folks wha's buried here used to think,' says he. ' But *es* it, sir ? ' says I. ' Iss, o' corse,' says he. ' Heaven all'ys ben down behind the sunset,' says he. An' then 'a walked off ; jawin' to 'es friends."

" Well," said Zeke, wistfully, gazing

away across the wide blue plain of waters to where the distant chain of islets stood out faintly on the horizon, "ef heaven es ovver there, I'd like to sail ovver to it. 'A must be some lovely plaace, doan't 'ee think so, Jimmy? We shud have enough to ayte there, an' no wan to clump* us. We cud go fishin' all day, an' be some happy, you!"

"Iss," said Jimmy, but with evident reluctance.

"Do 'ee knaw they want to taake us ovver to Maddern?" †

"Who towld 'ee so?" faltered Jimmy, with terrified eyes.

"I heerd Uncle‡ Mathey sayin' the cart was comin' to fetch us."

---

* Strike or beat.

† The Union Workhouse of the peninsula is situated at Madron.

‡ "Uncle" in the peninsula is not necessarily

" When ? "

" Dunnaw. But 'a said 'a was ordered. I'd raather go to heaven to mawther."

" So'd I," said Jimmy, now almost whimpering. " I doan't want to go to Maddern !" he cried, excitedly.

" Shall us borra Bill Polglaze's li'l punt an' be off?"

" Where to ? "

" Off to heaven, o' corse, ef 'tes ovver to Scilly."

" I'd like to spend me sexpence fust," said Jimmy.

" 'Spect there'd be shops ovver there like in to Penzaance.* We cud git wan o' the angels to shaw us ovver town."

a term implying relationship, old men and women are often called " Uncle " and " Aunt."

* Penzance is the chief town of the Land's End peninsula.

" That wed be bra' an' nice ! " said Jimmy.   " Iss ; le's go ! "

So the two children scrambled down from the cliff-top and stole across the beach to the little sandy cove where Bill Polglaze's boat was drawn up beneath the cliff.

It was a wonderful voyage : if they were never to have another, the memory of this one would last them for a lifetime.

The wide plain of waters, so superbly blue in the distance, pulsed around them in a glassy, green-tinged mass, as light and buoyant as their own thoughts. And when they glanced over the boat into the depths beneath them they could see the most exquisite patches and beds of colour melting into each other and making a very fairyland for the eyes. The white flutter of the waves at the foot of the cliffs, and across the Cowloes, the Shark's Fin, and other rocks in the vicinity, only served to bring out with added vividness the brilliant hue of the vast level plain. Even the rich, creamy foam that frothed around the Longships* was entirely robbed of its sinister significance by the hot and glittering sunshine and the placid beauty of the heavens, whose deep blue arch was unflecked by a cloud.

The wide-pinioned gulls wheeling buoyantly to and fro, even the low-flying sable cormorants, with their heavily-flapping wings and their awkward out-lines, were a delight to their eyes this delicious afternoon. And when the children descried an occasional 'school' of fishes, they fell to watching the

* The reef on which the Land's End lighthouse is placed.

roughening surface of the water, and the poppling and the tiny flashes of white, with an intent curiosity as insatiable as their wishes, for, children though they were, they carried humanity in their hearts.

"Ef we onnly had a line!" said Jimmy, regretfully. "I got a hook in me trousers'-pocket. Wish I'd spent me sexpence in a line!"

"'Spect the angels 'ull lend us lines," said Zeke, contentedly. "Thee can tell them thee got a hook : we cud git some fish for their brekfus."

"Do 'ee think God'll be like the p'leeceman," said Jimmy: "like that wan that come from Penzaance to taake-up faather?"

"No," said Zeke, decisively. "'Spect 'a'll be more like Mester Trenwith, what left us slaip in 'es loft an' gov us saffern buns.* I've heerd o' he afore : *He's* all right, Jimmy."

" Well," said Jimmy, dubiously, " ef he doan't taake me sexpence."

" He waan't do that," said Zeke. " He got more money, 'spect, than the Queen. Why 'es house es gowld from the hale to the spence ! "†

" I'm glad," said Jimmy. " So he waan't want me sexpence ; " and his hand dived into his trousers'-pocket to lovingly finger his solitary coin. " I'm rayle glad," said Jimmy, " I shall like He, b'leeve."

As they passed the Longships' reef, with its tall white lighthouse, the sun was flashing brightly on the panes of the lantern, and the children gazed at the structure long and curiously.

---

* Buns coloured with saffron, a dainty of the peninsula.

† From the entrance-hall to the cupboard.

" 'Spect weth their glasses* they cud see into heaven from there," remarked Jimmy to the Softie, as they left the reef behind them.

" Iss ; they'll see us an' be able to tell faather. When 'a come out o' clink†
p'raps 'a'll come ovver to us," added the Softie, wistfully, looking back at the reef.

" Mawther'll be there waitin' for us, o' corse," said Jimmy. " 'Spect she'll ha' tay ready 'genst we come, like she used to."

" Iss ; 'spect so."

" I'm hungry ; arn't thee ? "

" Iss : I cud ayte a mossel as thick as me fist."

" Well, we must maake haste ovver," said Jimmy. Then suddenly, " I caan't see the islands, can thee ? "

" No. But they're ovver there, right

---

* Telescopes.   † Prison.

'nuff," said Zeke. "We must raw more harder. Le's sing, shall us? P'raps the angels 'ull hear us an' look out for us."

And with that the two children began to sing at their shrillest :—

We're goin' home,
No more to roam,
No more to sin and sorra ;
No more to wear
The brow o' care—
We're goin' home tomorra !

Gradually, as the sun sank lower and lower, the waters around them seemed to widen in their loneliness and a chilling sense of fear began to awake in the children.

"Shall us go back, Zeke?" asked Jimmy, quiveringly.

"We mus be 'most got to heaven, I shud think," said the Softie, as he gazed up wistfully at the sky in the west, which was now one mass of glowing gold. "See,

Jimmy!" and he nodded his head towards the sky, "we caan't be far from the sunset, can us? An' down behind the sunset es heaven, the genelman said."

"I'm afeerd," said Jimmy. "I want to go back."

"Well," said Zeke: "but then we shaan't git to heaven."

"'Thee shall ha' haaf o' my sexpence; ef thee'll le' me go back."

"Well," said Zeke, with reluctant slowness. And with that they endeavoured to turn the boat's head shoreward; and evidently believed they had accomplished the task. For some time the swell had hidden the land from them, and, as the cliffs were invisible from the seats of the punt, they now took it for granted that they were rowing back to land.

Such a wonderful sunset they had never seen before. The enormous crim-

son flames that spread across the sky,
extending from the horizon to far beyond
the zenith, made a feast of colour so
superbly brilliant that the magnificence of
the spectacle awed them almost painfully,
and the two little castaways felt half in-
clined to cry.

Under the gigantic waves of flame, the
hollows of the swell became tinged with
vermilion, and the air seemed dazzlingly
full of gold.

" We must ha' got nearer to heaven
than we knawed," whispered Jimmy.

" I wish we'd gone on," Zeke sighed,
regretfully.

When the keenness of the rich, clear
colours began to fade, and to the crimson
and purple splendours overhead there
succeeded a wistful flush of violet, and
finally a faint and pensive lemon that over-
flowed nearly half the heavens, then the

children became aware that Fear was in
the boat with them, and their hearts
throbbed painfully under their ragged
little shirts.

At last there could be no doubt that
it was evening. In the east the moon,
that hitherto had been a phantom, began
to fill with light and glow silverly among
the clouds, and while the crests of the
long grey waves glimmered faintly, in the
dusky hollows it was certainly night.

The cormorants and gulls had winged
their way to the land; the sky, that all
day had been so blue and boundless, had
narrowed cruelly and now hung over
them with a scowl; and the children were
left with no other company than the
complaining wind and the great wan
moon.

Once they glimpsed a wandering
'school' of mackerel, that was making

a shimmer of silver drops amid the grey undulations; and at another time a band of ungainly porpoises passed so close to the boat that the children shrieked in terror, thinking the uncanny snorts were those of ghosts who were in pursuit of them. "Mawther! *mawther!*" little Jimmy screeched.

As the wind began to wail and sigh across the water, Jimmy whimperingly complained that he was 'steeving' with the cold. On which the Softie took off his own ragged coat and affectionately buttoned it around his little brother's neck.

Without knowing it, the children had drifted into the 'Chops' of the Channel —into the fairway of the unending procession of ships that rounds the wild Land's End from every point of the compass.

By this time all the lights of the
' Chops ' were burning brightly. The
fixed white light of the Longships' reef,
the alternate red and white flashes of the
Wolf, and the two fixed lights on the
dreaded Seven Stones : at no time, as they
drifted helplessly with the tide—which
outside the Kettle's Bottom was running
like a mill-race—were the children
beyond the range of one or the other of
these.

Their position was, indeed, one of the
most imminent danger. But the children
were cowed and numbed into apathy, of
which the torpor, happily, was heaviest
on their thoughts.

" Le's cuddle together, Jimmy ! " said
the Softie, gently. " It'll keep 'ee
warmer. Cuddle up to me ! "

And while Jimmy snuggled up against
the coatless Softie, the latter fell to pray-

ing in his uncouth fashion : praying till the big tears glistened on his cheeks.

Presently little Jimmy whimpered himself to sleep. But all through the night the Softie remained watchful, revolving in his dim and crippled mind the question whether God would send one of His angels to them, or whether, from the lonely crag of the Wolf, its terrible namesake would steal on them through the darkness, and its strong teeth would crunch them, bones and all, as a dog's white teeth might crunch up a rat.

Suddenly Zeke was aware of a deep, mysterious humming, coming towards him from somewhere out of the night.

"The Wolf! the wolf!" he screeched, in his terror, vainly trying to wake up Jimmy.

And at the same instant, something took shape amid the greyness, and he perceived a huge, black cliff towering high above him.

A second afterwards the heavy iron steamship was ploughing her way steadily through the long grey swell, her portholes gleaming, and her lights twinkling merrily, and her great screw churning the water into foam. But in the deep black hollows of the pitiless ocean Zeke and Jimmy were struggling frantically, the water choking in their throats.

In the darkness neither could see the eyes of the other, but they clung together tightly, so precious was the human clasp.

And in this way, paralysed and speechless with terror, they sank down into the vast abyss.

THE MAN AND THE MONSTER.

THE MAN AND THE MONSTER.

WHILE he was a child they concealed from him the existence of this Monster, of whom his parents stood in awe and to whom he himself was born a thrall. His parents, he imagined, held the strings of the universe, and according as they whispered so the heart of God was swayed.

But when he grew older he became aware of forces not to be propitiated even at the hearthstone, and especially of a shadowy Something in the background— some gigantic presence, some monster— of whom everyone stood in fear.

"I should like to see this monster face to face," he thought.

He implored his parents to let him face it ; but they dissuaded him affectionately.

"Not yet," said the father: and the mother echoed, "Not yet."

"You will have to face and wrestle with him presently," they assured him. "He stands waiting for us by the wayside, and his fetters few of us escape."

"Then have *you* met him, mother?" asked the lad, incredulously. "And you, too, father?"

And his parents answered "Yes."

"And do you wear his fetters?" And the little fellow looked them over from head to foot.

The father glanced at the mother, and, as he did so, he sighed deeply. And the mother, remembering many things, could only murmur, "Yes."

The lad was astonished and greatly pained. This Monster, then, had grieved and annoyed his parents! Very well, when he met Him he would have this to avenge. The World should see he could remember! And he thrilled at the thought.

" Ha ! ha !" laughed the Monster, who had overheard the boast: "you think of the World already, young master, do you? Possibly we shall not meet as strangers, after all."

At last, when he was grown to manhood, Nathan was one day going towards the house of his sweetheart—who was a woodman's daughter living at the edge of the forest—when he was staggered by a sudden blow dealt him between the eyes.

"Better *think* before going farther ! " said a hoarse voice close to him. " Why make a fool of yourself? What will the world say?"

"What do I care for the world!" cried Nathan, angrily, as he turned and fronted his insolent opponent. And immediately he was aware that it was the Monster he had so often heard of who now stood here barring his path.

"Who are *you*, that you should dare to meddle with *me?*" cried Nathan, passionately.

"I don't argue," said the Monster, "that's a simple waste of breath. But you'll not pass me without wrestling with me: and the one who wins rules the roast."

So they began to wrestle together at the edge of the wood.

Such a wrestling as this Nathan had never before experienced: it was a wrestling with the muscles and with the nerves, and with the brain most of all : a wrestling that at last bewildered him so completely that in it he almost lost grip on his identity, and the very forces of the universe seemed leagued against him for his defeat.

The air around them, as they fought, seemed full of voices—so craftily could the Monster manipulate his tones—and the background of the neighbouring forest, by a touch of magic, seemed no less than the vast panorama of life, with its myriad appeals to the memory and the imagination, its seductions for the eye and its flatteries for the heart.

And now Nathan was certain that this Monster he was wrestling with was some potent magician, not a mere mortal man.

One fetter after another the Monster threw over Nathan, and to break through them all seemed a task beyond his strength.

There was a chain woven of the hair of his father and mother, and since the hairs seemed alive and endowed with minatory voices, how could Nathan have the heart to break through this?

There was a chain composed of books, and these the volumes most treasured— and there was a chain of golden coins that chinked temptingly in his ears.

No sooner had Nathan burst one of the chains asunder than it was either pieced together or the pressure of the others was increased.

Nathan could not understand it: he was wrestling with more than the Monster —he was wrestling with his own moods and sentiments as well. And he had a traitor lodged within him who was always urging him to submit.

In vain Nathan tugged at, and writhed around the Monster; he was struggling with Colossus, and could move him not one whit.

Worst of all, he could not even elude him and take to flight. Once prisoned in that clutch he was prisoned beyond escape.

His brain reeled as the panorama swept distractingly before him, where he should only have seen the crowding trees of the forest: and the whisper of the many voices, and the straining pressure of the fetters . . . . he was unable to contend against them and against the traitor in his heart.

"I can't . . . . I give in !" he gasped, suddenly growing limp.

"You were bound to give in some time," growled the Monster, carelessly. "But take a peep at yourself in that pool yonder, friend. You will find you have been wrestling with me longer than you thought."

Nathan stooped to scan his features, and lo! he was grey and wrinkled. A cold shiver ran through him. " Have I lost so much of life!" he groaned. " And what have I gained in exchange?" he asked, dazedly, his eyes fixed on a band of mourners who were slowly bearing a coffin through the wood.

" Nothing that I know of," laughed the Monster, " except wrinkles and a ragged coat."

" And who *are* you, after all?" asked Nathan, gazing up at him. " I thought someone whispered your name to me just now."

" And what did they tell you I am called?" quoth the burly Monster.

" *Fate !* " whispered Nathan, seating himself heavily on a bank.

" A big name that," said the Monster, laughingly. " I could be content with a cheaper one. How do you like *The World ?* "

" Then I was a fool to wrestle with you," said Nathan, dejectedly ; his eyes still watching the vanishing band of mourners.

" Very likely," said the Monster : " but now that I have conquered you . . . . Don't stand mooning like that, man ! Here ! buy a coat."

EGO SPEAKS.

EGO SPEAKS.

Fragments of a confidence.

I.

THE dear, dear Earth, our mother and protector, who feeds us with the known and establishes our strength with the familiar, who is always with us whoever leaves us, and who holds our bodies till they are dust : her attractions for us are infinite and her love is inexhaustible : she is our dear, dear mother, and we are her children to the end.

But when Death's lean fingers finally close upon us and the familiar swiftly and irrevocably recedes ; when the sensations are unravelled and the weft of them ruined fatally, and the consciousness crumbles drowsily and the heart stands still ; ah ! then, when the soul is flung out into the darkness, what Power is there that shall comfort us, and to what shall we gravitate in our need ?

II.

I pass over the maddening agony of my murder. To lie there helpless in the darkened lane and have the life beaten savagely out of my body, was an experience grim and appallingly gruesome. The tramp, to whose greed and ferocity I had succumbed, I would have murdered myself, had I only had the power. But my body lay there wrecked and dead : and the unseen Ego was adrift in the world.

The unfamiliar—the unfamiliar!—I had always hated it. I had no strength of imagination to array my sympathies in line with it, and no unsatisfied hunger that made me crave to pierce its core. I had always hated death for its secrecy and its strangeness, for the things it concealed and the new experiences it would compel one to: and here was I dead and the book of the familiar closed irrevocably!

If only annihilation might have followed the stoppage of the pulse!

III.

And now my grisly experiences began.

Up to the moment when the shrine of my personality was shattered, I had been a quiet, well-behaved, tax-paying citizen: a married man with a wife and a couple

of children, and with a small circle of
intimate acquaintances, whose respect, if
not their active affection, I was presumed
to have secured and retained permanently.

The Ego, as it finally was dislodged
from the body, had vitality enough to
take the world by the beard, so proud
and energetic and self-sufficient did it
seem. But even while it gathered up the
world in its glance, it was conscious of
a certain drain of vitality in less than an
instant after it was dislodged.

With the loss of its body it had lost
more than its protection : it had lost the
kernel and crown of its consequence as
well. And it seemed to me, unless I
misinterpret, that its health and strength
were not inherent, but depended on the
attitude of its fellows towards it, so that,
practically, from the moment it was dis-

lodged from its envelope it began fatally
to shrivel and collapse.

I watched the tramp empty and toss
away my purse, take my watch and chain
and scarf-pin and even the pencil-case I
carried, and then, with a grunt at the
smallness of his booty, he dragged my
body among the ferns that grew rankly
against the hedge and, looking around
hurriedly, took to his heels.

I was distracted with a multiplicity of
emotions. I wished to watch the body;
I wanted to dog the heels of the
murderer; and I desired to see my wife
to inform her of the deed and of where
she might find the body and of how she
might find the man.

Finally I decided to follow the
murderer for the present; lest the man
should escape my vengeance after all.

But, to my dismay, the man kept

steadily plodding onward. He had soon left the scene of the murder miles behind him, and evidently had settled down to an all-night tramp. He appeared to me to be bound for London, which was distant from here about fifty miles.

At last I gave up the wearying pursuit and rapidly flitted to the neat little villa which my consciousness had called *home* while it had a body at command.

A more lame and impotent conclusion to an errand had never befallen me in the whole of my experience.

I was absolutely powerless to do anything. There was I in the house, unseen and unrecognised, and unable to communicate, even in the most rudimentary fashion, with those who were nearest and dearest to me on earth.

To add to my bewilderment and appalling loneliness, the part which the

body had played in my life began to be
apparent to me at last. Without it I
found I was barred, most effectually,
from definite communication with those
still alive. I might manage in some way
to impress a consciousness—might communicate to it an indeterminate impulse,
or arouse in it a transient hallucination—
but the capture of the attention, as by
personal magic, I was henceforth
absolutely powerless to effect. Neither
through the eye, nor the ear, nor even
through the touch, could I manage to
impress a being still alive. And shut out
from communication by any of these
avenues, I found myself now as impotent
as a dream.

Once or twice I managed to arouse in
my wife a casual uneasiness as to my
prolonged absence. But she was a placid-
natured woman, not in the least senti-

mental, and in the cosy domestic atmosphere the husband was not missed.

In vain I endeavoured to directly reach her thoughts : to convey to her some definite, unmistakable idea, such as a man may convey by a phrase or even a glance. She leaned back in the arm-chair dandling her infant placidly and cooing to it in the most matter-of-fact way in the world.

The sense of my isolation, and of my absolute helplessness, was an experience far more appallingly cruel than you who are alive can in any way comprehend.

The expulsion of the Ego from its battered fleshy tenement, grisly though it was, was less gruesome than this. To be a helpless sheaf and tangle of memories, with nothing but the fragile knot of consciousness to bind them into a temporary whole ; and to feel the knot

loosening and the sheaf falling asunder—
falling into a ruin profound and irreme-
diable—this, indeed, was the very bitter-
ness of death. I would have welcomed
instant annihilation as a boon.

As the hours lengthened my wife grew
restless, and by midnight she had at last
become thoroughly alarmed.

The next morning my absence had
grown portentous, and the police were
communicated with and set on the quest.

The body was soon discovered and
carried home : but the murderer had by
this time escaped securely, and—to make
a long story short—he still remains
uncaught.

IV.

At the funeral, so great was the
interest this aroused, Ego swelled with
life almost to its old dimensions.

The horses, with their plumes of feathers and their velvet trappings, paced slowly through the streets with the hearse behind them. Through the glass sides of the hearse one could see the long oak coffin resting on the shining brass supports and almost smothered in wreaths of hothouse flowers. But the dim form seated at the head of the coffin—the Ego from whom the veil had fallen for ever— this the living could not see, however closely they might look.

The streets were fuller, however, of dead folks than they were of the living, and the former, as they glided along dumb and invisible, glanced sadly at the wan and marrowless figure and bowed their heads to it as those who understood.

The journey through the noisy, crowded haunts, from which I was now for ever exiled, was a time of strange experiences as I sat crouched on the coffin. To think the bounds of my knowledge were enlarged so inconceivably, yet I was crippled so fatally and cut off cruelly from so much !

I was taking my last tithe of interest from humanity. This drive through the streets in the awful solitude of the hearse, with the trappings on the horses and the wreaths on the coffin . . . . and then the pit in the graveyard for the abandoned body, and for the spirit the vast black pit of the past!

V.

When the funeral was over and the murder had become forgotten—swept out of memory by the press of other incidents —Ego found its life oozing steadily away.

My wife that had been—my widow that was—was fairly young and reasonably attractive, and before her year of conventional mourning had expired she was again a wife, and I was to her but a memory: and a very thin and bloodless memory too.

Even the children ceased to trouble much about "father" now they had a newer flesh-and-blood father to make pets of them : and Ego shrivelled daily, and is shrivelling still.

I had fancied, while I was still clothed with a body, that, if I were freed from the material thraldom of the flesh, I would roam about the world feasting hungrily on its scenes until I was thoroughly sated with whatever it had to offer.

But what are art and literature, or scenery however beautiful, to the unhoused Ego with no register for its experiences, with its capacities like slipping sand, and the walls of its treasure-house broken down? The experiences of the senses—how could I garner them? The experiences of the soul—wonderful and terrible though I know them—how could I store them up except in the terms of the senses? how could I hold them to ponder over? how could I share them if I wished?

I found the homeless Ego so helpless in itself—so dependent on those who had known of its existence and to whom alone it could turn for consideration—that I was practically rooted to the habitat of my memories; and only there, and along these lines, could I exist.

VI.

Today I am still feebly existent. Tomorrow I may be wholly forgotten: and shall have ceased.

JOANNA.

JOANNA.

EVERY one for miles around knew Joanna. She was a tall, sun-browned, shabbily-dressed woman, with freckled hands, "as brown as a toad's back," and with thick sandy hair that she stowed away carelessly and unattractively under a ragged straw hat. But her pale blue eyes were quiet and patient, full of mild resignation and "as open as the day."

She had an old grey donkey—as patient and harmless as herself—and she earned her living as a seller of griglan brooms*

* Heath brooms.

and scouring gard,* " hurts "† and black-
berries (in their season) being also among
her specialities.

Joanna lived up in the lonely " high
countries "—the forlorn stretch of treeless
moors in which the lesser hills unpictur-
esquely culminate—and she was only
known to the cottagers in the " low countries " as one among the many pedlars of
the district, though notable for her honesty
and her sparing use of speech.

After their fashion, the cottagers were
rather kind to her. Occasionally one
would give her an old patched gown, a
worn turnover,‡ or a discarded pair of
boots; and, as no one had ever seen her
with a new hat, the presumption was

---

* Decomposed granite, used for scouring pur-
poses.

† Whortleberries.

‡ A small shawl for the shoulders.

that her straw headgear was always obtained as a gift, or else by way of friendly
barter.

Joanna was very good to the poor ass
that she so stolidly trudged beside all the
year round. She was never known to
overburden him, or even to strike him,
and she would often wait patiently on the
lonely highway while Neddy cropped a
meal from the tall hedges or took a drink
from some narrow rillet trickling through
the grass.

Neddy carried a couple of coarse canvas
bags, slung one on either side of him
and filled with scouring gard, and on his
back were piled the purple-tipped griglan
brooms. Joanna carried a large, shallow
basket, filled with "hurts" or with black-
berries, according to the season, and sometimes with bunches of juicy elder-berries,
that were carefully disposed on layers of

ferns. Occasionally the basket would be filled with elder-blossom—which the cottagers used largely for making elder-tea for colds—or with a purple heap of sloes and "bullens,"* that were ultimately to be manufactured into home-made wines. Joanna was also an excellent knitter, and sometimes she would bring with her knitted night-caps and stockings, and even an occasional pair of mittens. But for these there was not a very remunerative sale, and as the production of them meant the outlay of a good many coppers— —often, in fact, as much as a shilling— Joanna could only indulge sparingly in speculations of this kind, and at such times she was always tremulously nervous till she had realized her capital and felt financially safe.

Of Joanna and her antecedents no one

* Wild plums.

knew anything. Even her surname, if
she had one, had been dropped by the
way. She was for the cottagers merely a
weather-beaten wanderer, apparently as
friendless as the ass that trudged beside
her and with scarcely more pleasure in
her grey and narrow life.

But in her tiny cottage on Boswavas
moor, almost in the shadow of the ruined
circle of Boskednan, and with the bosses
of Carn Galva towering blackly above her,
Joanna, though lonely, was by no means
unhappy.

All around her stretched the wide,
wind-harried moor. The heather grew in
vast, tangled masses, with stalks as thick
as a child's wrist, and the sturdy furze-
bushes were so compact and tall that in
places they were as high as a six-foot man.
All day long, in the hot sunshine, the
kites kept wheeling to and fro across the

moor and the finches and whinchats flitted gossiping above the tussocks, the weasels and brown stoats watching them the while. And Joanna, looking out on the landscape spread before her, would watch the cows in the distant meadows, and the smoke from the cottage chimneys, and, listening to the hooters* of the mines and music of the skylarks, would try to believe that she was as happy as the best.

Since the death of her mother, years ago, Joanna had lived alone in the little cob-walled† cottage with its single room and its dilapidated roof of thatch, and was content if she could get bread enough to stay her hunger and could manage to keep warm in spite of wind and rain. She slept on a heap of ferns in the corner of the hut, with her clothes and some ragged

---

* Steam whistles.   † Earth-walled.

old sacks for bedding, and in winter stopped up the chinks of her dwelling with ferns and heather as best she could. Her fuel, of which she was very sparing, consisted of turfs and furze, which she obtained from the moor, with an occasional gift of cinders from a neighbouring mine, and her food and clothing she obtained by peddling among the hamlets, scouring the moors around her cottage to obtain the necessary stock-in-trade.

It was a hard life, but she had never known an easier one: and Joanna, after a fashion, was content.

Her mother had been a *bal* girl* on the floors† of Ding Dong,‡ and Joanna was a little unwelcome "come by chance"—an

---

* Mine girl. † Surface workings.

‡ Ding Dong is the name of a well-known mine on the moor; it is supposed to be one of the oldest mines in Cornwall.

infant which no one in the mine would
father, though it had been whispered at
the time, among the other *bal* maidens,
that she was really the child of the captain
himself.

Joanna's mother had died when her
daughter was about forty, and from that
time Joanna had lived absolutely alone;
unless Neddy, the ass, who lived on the
moors around the cottage, should be considered, under the circumstances, as con-
stituting a companion.

The winter, just past, had been a hard
one for Joanna : how she had kept alive
through it she would have found it difficult
to explain. In fact, if the strict truth
must be told, she had been compelled to
do a little shame-faced begging among the
distant hamlets between Morvah and St.
Just : having, even in this dire pinch of
necessity, found it impossible to summon

up sufficient courage to beg in the villages through which she ordinarily peddled.

At last, however, Spring was approaching. February, with its cruel blasts, was over, and March was now more than a week old. The grass had already begun to sprout on the hillsides, the thorns were budding beneath the sheltering carns, and here and there a patch of gorse was in blossom. As Joanna stood at her door in the morning she could hear the bubbling, liquid trills of the skylarks, and occasionally the song of a solitary yellow-hammer rippled around the cottage from the bushes in its rear.

She was thinking that soon she might be able to get a few days' work among the field-hands down in the lowlands at Gulval—her mother having made her promise, most solemnly, that she would never take a job on the floors of the mine

—and in this way she would be able to "rub along" through a week or two, until she could start again on her rounds through the little rain-sodden hamlets.

Suddenly, however, there came an unexpected change.

As Joanna looked out across the moor one morning, she became aware that the world was full of gloom. That the wind was high she had known all night, so loudly had it screamed and wailed around the cottage ; but she was unprepared for the sullen threatenings of the heavens.

The distant bay, which lay far below her eyry, was almost indistinguishable in the portentous shadow, and Joanna felt a growing sense of discomfort : it was so lonely up here in the heart of the gloom.

She suddenly wished that she had neighbours near her ; that she had friends of some kind—that she was anything except alone.

How terrible it would be (she thought, with a shudder) if she should one day die alone in her cottage : alone with the vague white face of Death !

Her heart grew heavy, and there was trouble in her eyes.

All the morning the wind kept steadily rising, till at last it had increased to a whole gale. The world was as dark as if it were sundown in December, and the air was so full of the rush and roar of the wind that Joanna, pressing her face against the window, was almost terrified at the wild hurly-burly round the house.

Presently thin flakes of snow began to appear, driven before the wind like fine white spindrift. In a little while the world was seamed with white wrinkles, and clots of snow began to cling to the bushes and boulders, the whirling flakes thickening in the air all the time.*

Soon it was impossible to see through the window-panes, the flakes were plastered up against them in such compact white scales.

Joanna unfastened the door to go out and scrape the panes, but the pressure of the indomitable wind was so great that, when she drew the bar, the storm almost hurled her off her feet. So persistent and savage was the roaring assault that, although she at once endeavoured to close the door again, she was unable to accomplish the task, try as she would.

She could scarcely believe the evidence of her own senses. And even while she was straining and tugging at the door— pulling at it with her hands, pressing

---

* This was the great blizzard of the 9th March, 1891.

against it with her body—the snow was whirling about her and almost blinding her, and there was a drift across the floor nearly half a foot deep.

Again and again Joanna tried to close the door : but the pitiless blizzard was far too strong for her. The earthen walls of the cottage were plastered with the flakes, and they even made a sputtering lodgment on the hearth.

Joanna's despair was terrible, and tragic in its intensity. The tall, gaunt woman, in her sodden garments, stood in the middle of the cottage knee-deep in snow, the flakes clinging to her dress and clotting on her hair, and the wind buffeting her and stinging her with its icy burden till she felt her heart was bursting and she could scarcely draw her breath.

The fury of the wind, here on the uplands, was so appalling that its uproar alone was sufficient to unnerve one; and when the storm began at last to strip the creaking rafters and she was aware that the rotten thatch was being torn away like paper, Joanna fell on her knees in the thick white snowdrift and wailingly buried her face in her hands.

She had lived alone and had tried to be contented. But to die alone—in *this* way. Oh, it seemed hard!

She could have wept for herself: but the tears were frozen on her lids.

She was afraid—she was afraid!

Was it Death that crouched in front of her, with such a pinched white face and with such blackness in his eyes?

The world was full of people—oh, would *no one* succour her?

If the wind would 'go to lie:' if the snow would only cease!

She fell to sobbing in her helplessness
. . . . she was so weak she could merely
moan. At last the silence of exhaustion
supervened.

Across the roofless cottage the wind
howled exultantly and the snow fell
thick and fast between the rafters.

Night came down as Joanna lay here
exhausted—the great brute Night that
sees and knows so much—but Joanna
did not tremble now to look in its eyes.
Her own eyes were glazing : her ears
were already dulled. What she saw was
not the dense and menacing darkness,
but the vast green moor as she had
known it in summer, with the finches
twittering across it and the sun gleaming
in the distance . . . .

The snow deepened above her body.
Joanna was at rest.

CALLING OF THE SEA.

THE CALLING OF THE SEA.

YES, it was verily Spring at last!

The grass was starred with brilliant yellow dandelions, and at the foot of the hedgerows the primroses were in flower. Never had the thickets been fuller of music; in the furze bushes the finches were as merry as crickets; and the sky— how immeasurably wide it seemed—was as blue as the eyes of a little sinless child.

From the shoulder of the huge, grass-clothed hill, where he was engaged in watching a flock of sheep, Elias was aware of the enormous plain of the ocean,

with its gleams of romance in the guise of
fleeting white sails, and its whisperings
and mutterings of incomprehensible
tragedies in the roar of its billows and
the wandering moan of the wind. And
the lad's heart swelled within him at the
vision : he desired, above everything, to
be out on yonder plain, with the waves
dancing under him and the wind
whooing in his ears.

Often—especially in the early mornings,
or in the narrowing twilight when night
was stealing across the hills—he had the
fancy (who shall say if it were only a
fancy ?) that he could hear the voice of a
maiden calling to him softly from the
sea : calling, calling, ever calling to him
wistfully, " *Come ! come ! come !* "

The line of the horizon was the gateway of paradise for him. If he could
only reach that line and pass beyond the

gateway, how the world would widen out
and unroll itself before him! and how
happy, how inconceivably happy he
would be!

He would sit for hours watching the
sails gleaming in the sunshine, or the
black smoke trailing behind the thin-
bodied steamships, that crawled like tiniest
toys along the edge of the horizon,
though he knew them to be veritable
monsters of the deep, with the strength of
a thousand giants gathered within their
ribs.

Oh, if he could only become a sailor!
If he could only discover the world
through the gateway of the sea!

And still, in the grey, mysterious
gloaming, or in that eerie hour between
the dark and the dawn, the voice came
crying to him, plaining to him across the
waters—crying to him urgently, passion-

ately, seductively; plaining to him with the wistful yearning of a maiden— " *Come! come to me! Come! come! come!* "

There was, however, here no harbourage for vessels—it was merely a long, bleak peninsula with a sheer wall of cliffs, and with skerries and reefs sown thickly along its shores—and Elias could only see the sailing-vessels and steamships passing to and fro at the edge of the world, or the brown-sailed fishing-boats creeping lazily along the coast.

To get a berth in a ship from here was impossible: they were all peasants or fishermen on the little wind-beaten peninsula, and Elias must either take up one of these primitive occupations, or must shoulder his bundle and set off to seek his fortune in the great hungry world that lay beyond the hills.

At last he could no longer withstand
this call that so haunted him. He slung
his bundle across his shoulder and set off
for the nearest port.

But when he arrived at the port—it
was a small and sleepy one—the tiny
tidal harbour had not even a coasting
schooner in it. There was nothing beside
the quay but an un-decked fishing-smack,
beached in the mud and now being
tarred.

So Elias, for the nonce, had to seek
work in the town; and presently he
obtained a job as carter to a coal-merchant, who had come from the hamlet
where Elias had been born and, for
this and other reasons, felt attracted to
him.

In this quiet little seaport—if such it
could be called, for not more than two or
three coasting schooners called there in

a month—Elias had now to content himself with his daily drudgery, and to wait
as patiently as he could for the fulfilment
of his hope.

When he had to turn his back on the
sea to drive inland among the hamlets, his
heart would grow as dull as a storm-
darkened landscape when the birds retreat
to their coverts and the wind begins to
moan.   But the homeward journey, with
his face turned seaward, was like the
joyous anticipation of a festival; and, as
he drove along the highway, he would
feast his eyes on the sea-line and, as often
as not, would carol like a boy.

Presently above his horizon rose a fair
young face—that of the coal-merchant's
winsome daughter—and Elias began to
experience the world-old trouble; hungering and thirsting after the mirage called
love.

The new desire, for the present, drove out the old one, or, rather, suppressed its keener manifestations ; and Elias went a-wooing and thought of little besides.

The girl was very human, and not un-reasonably coy, so that in a little while Elias was an accepted suitor, and by-and-by, in due course, he obtained possession of his bride and they set up house to-gether in the little hamlet by the sea.

Soon, however, the novelty of the situation wore off.

The girl was a good girl, and a very loving one ; but the man had listened to a voice sweeter and more seductive than hers : and the old longing began to haunt him more insistently than ever.

He was in love with the wide blue spaces of water with their ever-changing expression and their never-ceasing " cry ;" and he envied the gulls and the cormorants and the wandering shoals of fishes with an envy now sharpened into actual jealousy, so human was his love and so imperious its demands.

As he lay awake at night by the side of his wife, the wind that growled in the chimney, or rattled the loose-fitting window-frames, seemed to be growling angrily at him that he should remain a mere shore-limpet instead of launching out boldly on the vast unquiet sea. And the huge billows thundering against the cliffs below the cottage—he could feel their *thud, thud, thud,* as he lay here in bed—seemed endeavouring to reach him, to obtain possession of him by violence, that they might bear him off on their shoulders into the dim unknown.

At last this longing of his became an uncontrollable passion. On shore he could no longer live, that was certain.

He pined to have the keen, salt smell in his nostrils, and around him the heaving world of waters, with the white sails bellying-out above him and the ocean flowing past, like a mill race, as they ran.

One day, while in this mood, he suddenly disappeared.

His wife sought long and earnestly for him : but never again did the sight of him gladden her eyes.

From time to time she heard vague, flying rumours—faint, hearsay gossip as reliable as that of the swallows—to the effect that some such man as Elias had been seen here or there, in the Atlantic or in the Pacific, or had been heard of as wrecked, or as on such-and-such a ship.

Nearer than this to him, however, the wife could never get.

Once there reached her a rumour averring that Elias had been seen living in a state of semi-savage freedom on one of the warm, opulent South Sea islands : a mere narrow reef of coral, with the vast surf hammering against it incessantly and the sea-birds clamouring across it all day long.

But the truth or falsehood of this she was never able to determine.

He had deserted his human wife for the siren-voiced Ocean ; and the Sea, having once obtained possession of him, kept the secret of her lover, as such voluptuous creatures will.

THE VALLEY OF VANISHED SUNSETS.

THE VALLEY OF VANISHED SUNSETS.

MR. WHITEHEAD was very weary, and, it being Sunday afternoon in the middle of summer, he sat in the garden beneath the trees and watched the sunshine on the grass, glad to have an opportunity to rest without reproach.

The bees were droning drowsily among the tall holly-hocks and the light breeze, drifting above the garden wall, rippled among the leaves at the tips of the branches till their multitudinous fluttering made a music of its own.

At the other end of the garden, where

there was a long grass plot, two of his children were playing cheerfully together, and Mr. Whitehead, sitting here restfully in his chair, watched the children wistfully, and fell a-musing as he watched.

In Mr. Whitehead's brain, this hot afternoon, there was a buzz and pressure of thoughts that made his weariness almost excessive : it was as if the traffic of the streets—its pedestrians and its vehicles—were rumbling, rattling, trampling through his brain, making the walls of that theatre quiver and ache.

Then he thought of the dingy little office in which he had worked so many years ; of the faces that had come and gone at its desks since he had first planted his stool in the corner ; and of the dreary, dreary drudgery of its tasks.

And with that he remembered that when he left Heacham for London he had imagined to himself that life in the vast metropolis would be full of appetising pleasures and crammed with variety ; an existence full of colour and as satisfying as heaven.

But how few of his anticipations had he been able to realise !

He had been to a theatre once or twice, and he had made acquaintances— half-a-dozen or so—and he had seen an exhibition here and an historical building there. But of the vast, humming life and of the buzzing pleasures of the metropolis he had seen comparatively little, and had sampled even less.

His daydreams of his life in London had proved utterly illusory. They were gone down into the " valley of vanished sunsets " with his dead.

And with that he mused drowsily to himself as he sat here, " How full of

men's memories must that distant valley
be! I should like to spend an afternoon
strolling through its scenes."

"No, dears, don't disturb him! Father
is sleeping," said the mother: and she
laid a handkerchief over his face to keep
away the teasing flies. "Come softly
indoors, mamma will tell you a pretty
story." And she took the little ones'
hands, and led them into the house.

"This, then, is the Valley of Vanished
Sunsets!" mused Mr. Whitehead, as the
gates swung open and he passed down
the dewy path.

Never was greener grass seen by any
man: it was like the long, lush grass one
rolled in as a boy.

Mr. Whitehead's thoughts freshened
and his gait grew elastic as the aroma of
the grasses drifted into the air.

Now, Heacham, with its green, softly·

swelling meadows and its broad, firm beach with the waters of the Wash in front of it, was surely as close to heaven as little thoughts could wish to get ! The sea-lavender in the marshes, what a joy it was to gather it : and the gulls on the shore, one could wonder at and watch them by the hour !

And here were the broad, silvery waters of the Wash stretching away shimmeringly in front of Mr. Whitehead, with the coast of Lincolnshire dim and grey in the distance, and Boston spire . . . . But was it the famous spire, or was it not ?

Talking of spires, here was the church with its ivy-clothed buttresses : one could see it from the hill-tops as one went courting in the summer evenings—and never kisses were sweeter than Jessie's in those dear, sweet days !

And Jessie was dead and buried . . . . he would visit her grave in the church-yard . . . . How the sea-wind moaned through the screen of bushes along the path !

Ah, there were too many graves that he remembered in that churchyard ! . . . . Would he ever, himself, lie at rest among its mounds ?

He had lived, and had married, and he was middle-aged and tired of everything. But, surely, to be thus tired was not one of his daydreams ?

And he lay down on the grass to rest and recall his thoughts.

" Father sleeps long," said the mother, bending over him.

But he will sleep still longer. It is his last sleep this.

LEAH.

LEAH.

MYSELF I never believed her to be a witch, though there were those in the village who set that name on her; and certainly she had a gift of *some* kind, as was proved in the end to the cost of one or two.

She was a splendid girl, though she had detractors even of her beauty. She had the finest figure I have ever seen, and her face was one of those that lead a man to make a fool of himself. She had large black eyes, extraordinarily full of life: they seemed to glow and dwindle and wax and wane almost eeriely: and their long silken lashes she could use to some purpose. More bewilderingly beautiful eyes I never looked into. It was as much as a man's soul was worth to fall beneath their spell.

While she was still growing up the lads of the village began to court her, and, girl though she was, she was like a woman at the game. I remember how she would play off one of us against the other, and, if need be, any of us against our sisters, with a cleverness that caused endless trouble amongst us, though at that time the significance of our moods escaped us and we only knew that Leah had made us quarrel again.

When Leah was sixteen she had a regular sweetheart : that is to say, one whom she appropriated wholly to herself, allowing no one else to share his attentions. She ran around with Alf for perhaps a twelvemonth, and then, without any seeming rhyme or reason, she threw him over and refused to have anything more to do with him.

After Alf was dismissed, several others tried to woo her, and she drifted around occasionally with one or the other of the young farmers : indifferently on her part, as was very manifest, though the young fellow themselves were in earnest to the finger-tips.

But none of them seemed able to capture her heart. She played with them and threw them over with the airy indifference of the coquette. Yet each of them felt certain—and it was this that gave the sting to their disappointment— that she had a hot and passionate heart, if one could only get at it : a heart that would stick at little, and that could fire a clod as easily as it could animate a coal.

The other girls of the village, envious of her wonderful and unaccountable success—for there was scarcely one of the young men of the parish whom she had not at some time or other made cheap and second-hand—began to spread the report that she frightened away her lovers through having a touch of the witch in her: some uncanny gift, or power, which, as soon as they became aware of it, the young men hastened to escape from.

But the chatter of the girls made no impression on Leah. She simply wiled away their sweethearts from under their very noses, and then, when she was tired of them, let them flutter back again.

When Leah was about twenty, the annual shifting of the Wesleyan ministers by the Conference brought to the village a young minister of about five-and-twenty, the Reverend William Ernest Green.

Leah was now in the very perfection of her beauty, with large, glowing eyes that seemed to pulsate with passion, and with warm red lips almost wickedly provocative —especially when she smiled and set the dimples in her cheeks—and the Reverend William was impressionable, and human to the core.

Of course, as the minister was young and unmarried, all the young women of the village began to set their caps at him.

There was quite an exceptional attendance at the chapel at every service, and the dressmaker and the milliner had their hands full of work. Some of the girls, in their eager rivalry, even trudged in to the nearest market-town, in order to surpass their competitors in smartness, as well a to be earlier in the field with all their arrows feathered. And the minister found himself treated like a little china idol, and, apparently, was very well pleased with his cult.

But while the other girls were humming and buzzing around their idol, Leah remained quiet and seemingly unimpressed. She made no attempt at adding to the smartness of her appearance—in colours and fabrics she had a strange, gypsy-like taste, and, whether in the roadway or in the chapel, she caught the eye with a certain inevitableness—and she attended chapel, if anything, a little more irregularly than before.

And yet, in spite of her indifference—assumed, or of intent—there soon crept through the village a little hissing rumour to the effect that the Reverend William had been seen walking down the village with her: walking with *her*, while with the others he had not walked at all!

True, the walk began and ended within sight of the cottages : and true, also, that it was not immediately repeated. Indeed, if one were *very* charitable, it might be construed as accidental. But, none the less, the buzz of gossip that followed the event was loud enough and spiteful enough to fill the social atmosphere for weeks. Evidently it reached the ears of the Reverend William, for the young minister was, in many respects, as nervous as a cat, and it was easy enough to see that he was greatly disquieted. That Leah heard of it of course went without saying ; the greater portion of the gossip being flung directly at her.

Presumably the minister learned the lesson it was desired to teach him, for the feelings of the marriageable sisters of the Society were not again lacerated by the sight of their beloved and guileless pastor parading the village in such questionable company; and the services were once more as crowded as of old.

But her companions, or, rather, her rivals, did not spare Leah in consequence. On the contrary, they teased her to the fullest limit that they dared—for there was that in her that set a limit to the daring of even the silliest—telling her that, for once, she had found someone who could see through her, and who was not to be entrapped, however wily she might be.

Leah smiled in their faces, a strangely irritating smile : not so much a smile of mere anger or defiance, as one that had in it a contemptuous belittlement of their opinions : a smile so gallingly sarcastic that the triumph of her eyes was doubly enhanced.

They averred that they could not understand her; she was as deep as the Bay of Biscay. She had some wickedness in her mind; they would be surprised at nothing that she might do.

But of this, of course, the Reverend William could know nothing. He was a guileless young man, and he had no wife to warn him. Oh, if he only had the sense to take to him a wife, how the Reverend Mrs. William would cherish and protect him! and how difficult Leah would find it to fascinate him, if he had a Reverend Mrs. William with him always as a shield! The marriageable young women (and some of the widows as well) felt that never before had they so longed to cherish anyone. Surely this longing was a call from heaven? Ought they not to see that it was obeyed?

Meanwhile the Reverend William preached as eloquently as ever, and all the females of his congregation watched with breathless attention to see in whose direction the balance of Fate would dip.

Leah had of late attended chapel very irregularly; in fact, she had not been there since the first Sunday in January—in the village they kept a close watch on matters of this kind—and it was now the second Sunday in March.

There was a fairly crowded congregation —the chapel being about three-parts full —and in front of the rostrum, and not a dozen yards from the preacher, sat Leah, with all the woman in her glowing in her eyes.

The Reverend William, as he stepped softly from the preacher's vestry to the rostrum, became instantly aware of her magnetic presence, and a swift, electric current seemed to tingle through his nerves as he glanced at her for a second and then hastily withdrew his eyes.

Never before had Leah looked so fascinating. The clear, soft curves of her face were most tempting. The minister looked at her clean-cut nostrils, the soft droop of her lips, the deep-lashed eyes, and her glowing magnetic beauty as a whole, and there surged through him a hungry impulse to seize her face between his hands and kiss it wildly and madly, kiss it defiantly before them all.

If he dared to ! If he only dared to ! If he could but summon up the courage to achieve his desire !

But, though the hot blood poured through his veins like lava, he thought . . . . and he knew . . . . and to the thinking and the knowledge he succumbed.

Leah wore an entirely new costume ;

town-made and very stylish ; and the eyes
of the females in the congregation looked
her over and over enviously.   In fact,
among the other girls and women in the
chapel — what   with   their   ill-fitting
garments and their defective taste in
colours, their lack of ease in attitude and
their want of beauty of line generally—
Leah stood out here with a distinction as
absolute as if she were an oddly beautiful
flamingo that had suddenly alighted
among the poultry in a yard.

The Reverend William felt disquieted
to the very centre of his being.   His
hands were moist with perspiration ; and
as he turned the leaves his fingers
trembled noticeably.

In the singing, Leah's rich, sweet con-
tralto seemed to pierce through the
intertangled mass of sounds with the
same unique effect as that with which

she physically dominated her neighbours: and the Reverend William, in order to taste her voice to its fullest sweetness, spun out the singing as long as he could. That he spun it out for her sake, Leah recognised very clearly; and she sang at him and to him with a witchery that overpowered him.

He gazed at her with an intentness, with a gaze so shamelessly fascinated, that the congregation quickly began to take notice of it, and the girls, who watched him hungrily, grew hot and breathed deep.

When the singing and prayer were over the minister seemed ill at ease. The first face he had glanced at, was that of Leah, who evidently had been quietly watching for his glance, and though Leah merely smiled with those wonderful eyes of hers, the Reverend William coloured violently and trembled in all his joints.

Finally, however, with an effort, he drew on the sources of self-control within him and managed to continue the service on its appointed lines.

For the portion of scripture to be read, he chose a chapter of the Song of Solomon, and his reading of it was a revelation to his congregation : a revelation of secret wishes in themselves as well as of secret wishes in their minister. They looked from one to another uneasily, endeavouring to catch, if they could, the significance of the changeful expressions around them, and more than one wondered how much she unconsciously might have revealed.

The atmosphere of the little building seemed full of undischarged electricity ;

there was a sense of trouble and unrest in the bosom of almost everyone.

During the sermon, Leah fixed her eyes boldly on the preacher, who appeared to surrender himself absolutely to her glance.

It was less a sermon to the congregation than a discourse addressed to *her:* a discourse that, in the end, became a highly impassioned monologue, of which, although the phraseology was religious, the mood and attitude were as secular as the glitter in his eyes.

The Reverend William had advanced to the front of the rostrum, and stood leaning on, and half over, the protecting rail, gazing at Leah with an almost unwinking gaze: evidently absorbed beyond the prick of shame, and possibly absorbed also beyond the registration of his consciousness: for his fascination, evidently, was so deadly helpless that it might have been the effect of mania or of mesmerism, for all the freedom of volition discernible in the man.

Presently the congregation was literally shaken in every nerve.

"Leah!" cried the minister; and again, agonisingly, "*Leah!*"

"Come!" said Leah, sweetly, lifting her hand and beckoning to him; but never for a moment removing her eyes from his: "Come and sit beside me!" And then, imperiously, "*Come!*"

The climax of the drama was hidden from me by the sudden uprising of the congregation. In the gallery, in the body of the chapel, the people stood up excitedly in their seats: there was a rustling of dresses, a shuffling of feet, the sound of heavy respirations everywhere: and presently, when I again caught sight

of the minister, he was seated beside
Leah in front of the rostrum; the whole
congregation staring at him in horror,
while he leaned against Leah as if he
were asleep.

They tried to induce him to leave
Leah, but something was wrong with the
man. A spring had broken in his nature
somewhere, and he clung doggedly to her
side: not arguing with, or repulsing them,
but keeping dumbly to his seat.

Finally Leah rose up and fronted the
congregation. " It is a little village, this,
and you are little people in it. But you
thought you were the world and knew
everything, didn't you? With your hats
and your dresses you were stronger than
flesh and blood, you thought. But flesh
and blood wins after all, you perceive.
This man, here," and she waved her hand
towards the limp and pallid minister,

"you thought you could teach to flout me : you have succeeded, have you not? To be quite frank with you, I don't want him : he is too little of a man for *me*. He will suit some of you better : take him, if you like!" And, with a gesture of disdainful abandonment of him, Leah turned on her heel and contemptuously walked away.

They conveyed the minister to his lodgings and a critical illness ensued : an illness from which he emerged physically a wreck and with his head and face as bald as the back of his hand.

Leah had quietly left the village the morning after the minister's downfall : and I have never seen her since, from that day to this.

A DROLL RESULT.

"Out of this, you selfish dog!" thundered the father. "If I am unfit for work is that my fault? You would begrudge helping to keep your poor father alive, would you? You are no son of mine— you are the son of a dog! Begone!"

And the father, with his face red with passion, waved the young man angrily towards the door.

"But, father," began the sister, "Paul has always done his utmost——"

"Done his utmost! Then why does he talk of marrying, the scamp! He knows I am unfit for work, and his paltry earn-

ings—why, what are they? They barely
pay for his keep, and provide a mouthful
for you and I, perhaps. And yet——"
and he watched his son's eyes furtively, to
see if he could detect any signs of his
being cowed. "And yet," he burst out,
with renewed ferocity, "and yet he talks
of marrying—the selfish hound! Out of
this, you cur! No longer count me as
your father! It has been self, self, self,
with you all your life long!"

The young man opened the door and
went out.

"*Am* I so very selfish?" he mused:
and he walked dejectedly towards his
sweetheart's cottage.

As he drew near the house in the
narrowing dusk, he fancied he saw an ac-
quaintance of his pass from between the
door-posts and hurry down the lane. "I
wonder why Will went off without speak-

ing? Have I offended him too?" Paul mused, dispiritedly.

"I am in great trouble, Janey," began Paul, as soon as he saw her.

"What about, now?" asked Janey, indifferently.

"Father has turned me adrift. I think only of self, he says."

"And he's quite right there!" cried Janey, emphatically. "You think only of yourself—a truer word was never spoken! Here have we been engaged for three years now, and not a word of marriage, and no preparations for it. I tell you, I'm tired waiting for you: you're too selfish for me. It is all self, self, with you—nothing but self!"

And Janey flounced indoors with a very red face.

"It must be true, then," said Paul, "it is the verdict of everyone." And he walked away slowly; his head hanging down.

He daundered on, without thinking whither he was walking, until presently, when the darkness began to close him in craftily, he was aware that he had wandered into the heart of the moorland, where the wind kept keening all day long.

Deeper and denser grew the blackness around him, till at last Paul recognised that he was alone with Night—that sour old hag whose hateful embraces only the Devil can endure. "Ay, old mother, they all hate you," he murmured. "It must be for your selfishness they hate you : for what do you give to any of us ? The Day gives us light and warmth in abundance; it fills us with something—a touch of its own cheerfulness ; and it freshens our thoughts for us and gives us new ones of the best. But you, you close our lids, you make us drunken with slumber, and then you steal from us our thoughts and give us your black dreams in place of them. Self is *your* curse, too, old mother, as it is mine." And Paul's head drooped, as the criminal's who is judged.

" Who is that mumbling to himself? " asked a voice from the darkness.

Paul's hair stiffened in an instant, and his mouth gaped widely.

" What are you abusing mother for : you up there ? " cried the deep, hollow voice from somewhere out of sight.

Paul took to his heels and ran on any-how, till suddenly he stumbled and fell sprawling among the ferns.

" Well, and what do you want of me ? " cried a voice at his ear.

Paul attempted to rise, but there were

fingers in his hair, and bony fingers, he thought, on his throat.

He opened his eyes ; a Figure was bending over him : it was distinguishable as a deeper darkness amid the shadows— a formless something that could move and grip and speak.

" Well, and what do you want of me ? " asked the hollow voice.

" Nothing, that I know of, sir," said Paul, humbly : and gasped, and was aware of an oppression at his heart. How grueingly chill the night air was !

" You are burdened with too much self," said the Figure : " is that so ? "

There was a whispered, " Yes."

" I alone can heal you of that disease for ever ; " and Paul quaked in his vitals at the hollow voice. " I alone. Do you wish me to exercise my skill ? "

" No, no ! " wailed Paul. " I am not yet ready ! "

" You will never be more ready than you are now," said the Figure. " It is the same cry from all of you, young and old."

" Any way short of that ! " wailed Paul to the Figure. " Any way, any way short of that ! "

The fingers relaxed their grip and Paul's heart grew elastic. His blood began to leap ; he rose to his feet and ran on breathlessly.

" Where are you running to—you ? " cried a rough, cracked voice.

And Paul was aware of a little old woman coming along through the ferns with a lantern in her hand.

As the light of the lantern flickered on her features, Paul felt something like a qualm and shudder in his spine. Yet, that she was kin to him in some way, he was sickeningly aware.

"Ho, cousin! it is you, is it?" said she, with a grin of welcome. "What do you want out here on the moor after nightfall?"

Paul told her of his misfortunes, gasping out the words brokenly. "I want to get rid of the 'self' in me," he groaned.

"Only my brother can quiet that in you—once and for ever," said the little old woman, blinking up in his face. "I can strengthen it for you," and she leered at him confidentially. "I have done that for many men, and for many women too."

"No, no! Oh, no! I want to get rid of it!"

The old woman put her fingers to her mouth and whistled shrilly.

And Paul was aware of an exquisitely beautiful damsel coming towards him through the ferns, with her eyes fixed on his.

" If you are bent on folly, cousin, put your lips to my daughter's. Lady Folly she is, and folly she will teach you : no one is cleverer at the game," grinned the hag.

And she held up her lantern, peering up to watch their faces.

The damsel put her soft red lips to Paul's and the forces of his nature were subtly unknitted : his eyes lost their steadiness and his will turned awry.

And presently Paul found himself alone among the heather, with the grey dawn widening mysteriously overhead.

He stared blankly around him, feeling dazed and helpless : so bewildered and weak he looked, one would have taken him for a fool.

On he wandered aimlessly, he knew not whither, until at last he found himself within sight of the hamlet that he had left so disconsolately . . . . how long ago ?

And just then Chance came strolling along the roadway and asked what was the matter with him and whither he was bound.

Paul answered the questions meekly, telling him all that had occurred.

"Oh ho! is it so?" laughed Chance, and watched him jauntily. "You are just the football I want, my dear young cousin. Come, roll yourself into a ball, if you please!"

To the best of his ability Paul did as he was directed: and a pitiable object the poor fellow looked, crouching here

in the dust with such dejection in his
eyes.

"Now I am going to kick you," said
Chance, with a laugh.

"Yes," said Paul, not daring to dis-
sent.

So Chance began to kick him along the
roadway like a ball.

Into the sleepy village Chance kicked
him ruthlessly, and the villagers woke up
and began to laugh raucously: never a
bigger fool than this had they had to jeer
at in their lives.

Hither and thither Chance kicked the
fellow—into the tavern and out of it,
into the hedge and into the ditch, and
into every rat-hole or sewer-trap the village
held concealed.

A man with no self-respect, no sense of
self-regarding decency! why, the villagers
themselves began to kick him in con-

tempt. Such a thin-blooded, backbone-less creature they despised !

At last Chance handed him over to them entirely.

"You will keep it up better than I could," said Chance.

Presently, as the villagers were kicking Paul along carelessly, they came to the churchyard—and kicked him in there.

There was a pauper's grave newly dug in a corner, and, seeing the grave was empty, the villagers kicked him into that.

The old hag looked on leeringly from a mound. "He sleeps soundly; I should like to break that sleep of his," she muttered; "the game was over too soon;" and, as she thought of it, she laughed.

THE SORCERY OF THE FOREST.

K

THE SORCERY OF THE FOREST.

OF our ship's crew only three remained alive. That it was useless waiting here any longer was evident. It was now three weeks since we had been shipwrecked and in the interval we had failed to sight a single ship.

In front of us we had the limitless and lonely ocean, and the dense and gloomy forest rose threateningly at our back ; but we judged that somewhere beyond the forest—if we could only get through it— we should strike a part of the coast-line either inhabited by the natives or likely to command a view of passing vessels. So

we reluctantly decided to turn our backs
on the sea and win our way through the
forest if we could.

Dear God in heaven, what an experience that was ! As we plunged into
the vast green depths of the forest the
huge walls of vegetation shut us in completely. Before we had passed many
yards beyond the thickets at the out-
skirts we were in a world of trees : a world
alien and monstrous: a world which (however picturesque it may be to dream of)
was to our experiences uncanny to the last
degree. To be prisoned in a labyrinth of
vegetable monsters may sound pleasant to
the fancy : but it is to be prisoned none
the less.

I suppose we were what would be called
coarse men. Certainly, neither our tastes
nor our imaginations were unduly fastid-
ious. But the dense primeval forest with

its gloom and its monstrous growths, its
crawling, clinging, slippery vegetable life,
rankly full of sap and superabundant
moisture—its varieties of bestiality in
loathsome profusion, from snakes and
apes and ungainly vampire bats, to ants
and beetles swarming underfoot, and great,
hairy spiders swinging overhead—this atmosphere, these objects, oppressed our
consciousness like a nightmare : and the
thick, green dome that everywhere over-
arched us, became at last, to our sickened
fancies, like the ceiling of a vault.

The sense of insecurity, deepening into
actual fear, begotten by the stealthy
movements of the wild animals and of
the filthy brood of apes and monkeys,
was keen enough to take away half the
relish from our lives. The opulence of
the vegetation in no way charmed us, the
gigantic trunks and the infinite network

of branches, the apparently inexhaustible fertility of Nature (creating, as it were, in very wantonness in these secret, ancient haunts of shadow) disturbed us even to the point of nausea.

It was not of fair Greek goddesses with limbs of marble and with eyes of almost infinite witchery that we instinctively thought in these green recesses ; nor even of horned and bearded satyrs, with humanizing touches in their gambollings and pipings : one thought rather of the uncouth gods of the savages, swarthy forms gross-lipped and evil-eyed, with the appetites of animals and with bestiality in every limb. No nude black Venus cast her spell upon us here ; but rather the monstrous, lustful, cannibal imaginings that the man of the woods and of the swamp and of the horrible slime-pit has evolved from the foul black depths of his nature : and of these the creeping poison thickened in our blood.

We felt so feeble and helpless amid the exuberant vitality, that the foundations of our lives seemed broken up and destroyed. Right and wrong, and the ordinary con- ventionalities of life, lost their meaning and significance in this primitive and savage world, whose laws we entirely failed to comprehend. The latent brute in us began savagely to assert itself. Whatever experiences in our past had been sensual and unclean now set them- selves, as it were, in the very forefront of our thoughts and began to openly poison and demoralize our minds. We had entered the forest men—though sad and disheartened ones—but it seemed possible that, if these experiences continued, some power in its sombre fastnesses would filch from us our humanity and would sensualize us steadily to the level of the beasts.

Through the rank, thick undergrowth we made our way dolorously, feeding—with more than a touch of the savage—on anything and everything that seemed to us edible. We lived the lives of pigs rather than of human beings. Only the primal instincts seemed to survive in us : of everything else the sorcery of the forest had despoiled us : and in the vast green depths we were ignorant of our loss.

Things to interest us in the forest there undoubtedly were. The opulent vegetation at times awed us by its magnificence. The huge, columnar trunks with their enormous girth ; the twisted masses of parasites that hung from the branches, apparently strong enough for cables for a full-rigged ship ; the chaos of interlaced, fantastic grasses; the arborescent ferns, with their gigantic fronds ; and the startlingly vivid blossoms of the orchids, whimsical in shape to the point of grotesquerie, and almost inconceivably gorgeous in their hues : these occasionally caught our fancies with such suddenness of appeal that we gasped and stood breathless in inexplicable awe. The indescribable luxuriance of the mosses and crypto-gamia ; the lush, strange forms and fantasies of vegetation that made a world of mystery of the so-called undergrowth ; the weird green light ; the myriad voices of the forest—-the screams of parrots, the cries of monkeys, the roar of the wind along the roof—dear Lord ! these both gladdened and saddened us as we toiled onward : the little humanity that was left to us seemed transformed as well as cowed. We felt as helpless and insignificant as so many ants : and in a world as far removed from that from which we drew our memories, as if we had passed (through dissolution) into a world saddening by its strangeness, a world where our crudest and wildest fancies had been suddenly and bewilderingly transformed into facts.

The brilliantly-coloured birds brought us no comfort, nor the georgeous-winged butterflies, nor even the wandering bees. We were oppressed by the unfamiliar opulence and magnificence : we hungered for the familiar with a terrible famine in our hearts.

Cowed and frankly demoralized by our surroundings, how intensely we longed to see a human face !

At last one day, to our unspeakable relief, we were again confronted by a human visage.

In the apparently impenetrable heart of the forest we came across a cluster of about a dozen huts, in which resided some fifty or sixty savages; black, absolutely nude (male and female), and with a language that to us was wholly incomprehensible.

A life more rude and elementary we had none of us ever witnessed. But still, arrested though it was, the life was human in its basis, and my companions succumbed to it immediately and help-lessly.

I admit that there was a certain stealthy attractiveness in a life so primitive and free as this. There was even a fascina-tion in the dusky womenfolk : they were like the supple, tawny, passionate bond-slaves that occasionally form the fringe of a harem in the East.

One young female caught my fancy strangely : she was as lithe and active as the ideal gipsy, and had as hot and restless blood in her veins. Though black and nude and frankly sensuous, she had for me an odd, uncanny attraction, and here, in the dense green heart of the forest, it seemed possible to divine in her a wild black Venus, born of the torrid heat and the monstrous woodland and by no means free from the uncouthness of her origin, but with the quick, hot heart of a woman beneath her breasts.

After I had been living in the leaf-covered huts about a week, this girl and myself stole away together: creeping through the undergrowth, crawling stealthily through the grasses, the idea of a dual life magnetizing both.

The supple black figure that henceforth kept beside me—false, savage, a mere bundle of instincts and appetites—was at first both attractive and invaluable as a companion: but the crude and unrelieved sensuousness of her nature finally sickened me as the great, brutal forest had done.

The hourly companionship, so close and yet so narrow, at last became hateful and altogether unendurable. I felt I must escape from her, if I had to kill her to be free.

One night as she lay sleeping I fled from her in horror: and never since (thank heaven!) have I seen her dusky face.

*   *   *   *

My life has many memories that I scarcely care to linger over: but this of the forest is the most nauseating of all.

A PLEASANT GOSSIP.

A PLEASANT GOSSIP.

In the green heart of an ancient woodland three birds sat perched on the
massive limb of an elm-tree, gossiping
together in the shady afternoon.

Beneath them the forest ways were
paved with blue-bells, and through the
fresh green foliage, that formed a
canopy over them, the light filtered
restfully, as through the windows of a
cathredral.

It was early spring: and the green,
winding glades were full of music. The
thrush and the blackbird sang eagerly
against each other, the secret cuckoos

sounded their word of enchantment, and the wind purred lispingly as it slid among the leaves.

Many strange things have I seen, said the wood-dove, but the strangest of all I saw in the valley down yonder : a woman with a crown of thorns sprouting from her brow. For every grievous sorrow—and her cross had been a heavy one—a living thorn had pierced her brow and a drop of blood had left her heart. When I saw her, a complete crown circled her head, and her face was as bloodlessly white and waxen as that of one whom Death has frozen with his kiss.

A stranger thing than that I have seen, said the blackbird. I have seen a lad whom Nature, in a freak of cruelty, created as a mere fleshly husk without a soul. But his mother, in her loving kindness, that the hope of heaven might still hearten him, bestowed her own soul on him—such tenderness has a mother— and, with this soul within him, the lad is growing to a noble man.

The woman with the crown of thorns and the lad without a soul, were mother and son, said the wise old raven.

A stranger thing than either I have seen, said the raven : I have looked in the eyes of a man escaped from hell. Down by the sea-shore yonder there is a winding cavern that pierces right through the heart of the solid granite cliffs, and reaches to the pitch-black lips of hell. Through this cavern a lost soul crept from tor- ment : and there I saw him—scarred, and black, and wolfish—glaring out wildly at the tossing leagues of water. He had crept up from hell to the cold and restless sea to cool himself again in its enfolding waters and to see once more the vast grey spaces that he had loved so keenly when the heart within his breast was still of flesh. But no one may permanently escape from hell. Ere nightfall the Old One had gripped the man again. The sight of the dear familiar sea for a few brief seconds, and a momentary glance, through the darkening window-panes, at the face of his wife, to whose cottage he had made his way—and then the fingers of the Old One closed over him stealthily. Ere the sun—a red ball at the horizon on his arrival—had become a thin line of crimson, just dipping out of sight, I saw him again haled back through the cavern to hell. Eyes more full of despair—unutterable, unendurable—I have never seen, *never!* said the wise old raven. Of the woman with the crown of thorns this was the husband.

She lies now in her coffin, said a robin, who had been listening.

That is well for her, said the raven to his gossips.

THE VEIL OF MÂYÂ.

THE VEIL OF MÂYÂ.

I.

"Shall I bestow on them this veil?" asked the gracious Presence.

The parents glanced at the babes slumbering peacefully on their mother's knees, and the father stroked his beard as he mused on the question.

"Would it add to their happiness?" the mother asked, wistfully.

"Would it cripple their power to gather knowledge?" quoth the father.

"I have only the veil to bestow," said the Presence. "Its value or its worth-

lessness they must discover for themselves."

"Let my little daughter wear it," the
mother whispered, lovingly.

"I reject it for my son!" said the
father, emphatically.

"So be it," said the Presence.   Then,
flinging the mysterious veil over the
daughter, she laid her back in the
mother's lap and suddenly disappeared.

II.

The children were as subtly diverse in
character as if there were a racial chasm
between them : or as if one had been fed
on the honey of fairyland and the other
on the coarser fare of the trolds.

For the little girl the garden was on the
very skirts of Paradise.   Playing in its
walks she could see the tiny, speckled

gnomes hiding in the velvety bells of the foxgloves, and in the vibrant twang of the bees among the honeysuckle she could hear the bugles of the little fairies who were playing among the flowers.

The soft evening clouds, floating lightly along the blue, were the flowing robes of angels who ran playing across the sky : and the vast red sun, just glimpsed between the heights, was a great red giant glaring over the hill-tops ere he finally laid himself down to sleep.

Music the child held as the very voice of God. Its melting strains made wet her little eyelids, and to its joyful notes her feet danced lightly. But when it grew grave, and uttered deep, solemn melodies—ah! then it was the dear Father grieved in some way, and her little heart would throb with a sympathetic ache.

As she grew up, men and women were always beautiful and wondrous to her. The bowed and wrinkled peasant, to whom the idea of rest was soothing, and the lady, fretted with idleness and as graceful as a flower—they were both of them her sisters, and the pressure of either's hand was sweet.

The traffic in the streets was not the movement of men and women who were bent on business and spurred mainly by the impulse of their needs, but the roaring flood of life solemnly beating out its music in harmony with the vast and grander music of the spheres.

The church was the most precious and most sacred of symbols: she could feed her heart within its precincts in a hundred different ways. And pulpiteers and medicine men, the wranglers in the courts and the licensed fighters, all the brigades

that wear uniforms she admired most pro-
foundly.

So closely did the veil of Mâyâ hang
before her eyes.

III.

But the brother in the flowers sought
for the pistils and the stamens, and
ferreted out in the trees the structure of
their leaves and the slow and painful cir-
culation of the sap. For him there was
no dryad in the trunk of the oak-tree, but
only the juices of the earth and the nutri-
ment of the sunshine built into the sylvan
monster and traceable in its cells.

The church, with its ritual, had grown
up around the altar, as the house, with its
domestic economy, had grown up around
the hearth : and the central stone of the
one, in spite of the embroidery of its

keepers, was no whit more divine than the central stone of the other. The bishop in his black apron, and the cook in his white one, they were allied in occupation and were on an equality in their cult.

The streets were full of combative human beings, each man hungering and thirsting for the satisfaction of his needs. And society was not something inexpressibly beautiful, devised and preordained by the wisdom of a god : it was a mere affair of balance, with weights that were fraudulent in their denominations and with blind Chance constantly meddling with the beam.

IV.

Every one loved and admired the girl, and when she grew to womanhood she had suitors by the dozen, and the glamour of love was heavy on her heart.

Her parents being dead, she married a gay young officer whose exterior and manners had fascinated her strongly. From the charm of these she divined that his heart was as an angel's—as unspotted as a lily and as innocent as a child.

In vain her brother had endeavoured to dissuade her from this folly: she had been told so often that he was a mere blind materialist, that it seemed to her that here his judgment must be worthless.

" I am sorry to differ from you on this point," said she: " but I feel that here I must obey my heart."

Tom shook his head sadly. " You will find it merely flesh and blood."

" Is love nothing more, then, than a matter of cells and molecules ? "

Her brother wisely held his peace.

Meanwhile Tom in the great orchestra of life had with difficulty been finding his instrument and his note. And now that these were found he sat down to play his part. No illusions did he cherish—not even as to himself—men were men and women women; and the pit of death was deep.

V.

The years sped on and Ellie was a broken-hearted woman.

Her husband, thinking more of life's pleasures than of its duties, had made many perilous steps, and at last had made a fatal one. A week ago "the honourable and gallant gentleman" had been sentenced at the Old Bailey for a most heartless seduction, and he now wore a suit with the broad arrow stamped on it, instead of the gaily-coloured cloths and embroideries of his trade.

And to-night poor Ellie, with this shadow hanging over her, lay helpless under the curse of Eve.

VI.

Death sat in his gloomy watch-tower in the belfry, where the dust was thick and the bats hung in clusters, and looked sadly down on the rain-beaten graves.

Presently he conned his fatal list of names.

" To-night the twins ! " he muttered in his beard.

Then with heavy steps he descended from the belfry and passed out into the slowly-gathering gloom.

" The veil of Mâyâ I shall strip

M

from her at last!" muttered he; and a sombre fire began to smoulder in his eyes.

But, behold! another Form was in the room before him : the grave and gracious Presence that had bestowed on her the veil.

"She will pass with the veil wrapped closely around her," said the Presence to the grim black Shape as he entered.

And as Death laid his hand on her heart and froze it, he was aware that through it all the veil floated before her vision, and in it she saw heaven, and through it she saw her god.

"To the last the prey of illusions!" muttered Death.

"Even *your* coming it has sweetened for her!" said the Presence.

"Has it?" said the Shape: "you

will see if her brother will tremble at me. Yet the veil of Mâyâ has never shrouded *him*."

To the brother's room went the Shape, and laid its hand upon his brain.

"So the end has come, then—the end thus early!" And Tom drowsed in his chair, and as he drowsed he dreamed confusedly; the life flickered out, and in the chair he lay a clod.

VII.

As Death climbed back to his lair in the belfry and lay down in the darkness in the thick, foul dust, he mused perplexedly on this veil of Mâyâ, of which men think so much but which counts for so little in the end.

"With, or without it, there is life: and with, or without it, all must face me.

Has it any use, then, after all?" mused Death.

And with that he fell asleep, leaving the question still unsolved.

JOEL.

JOEL.

To the west of the village, ever confronting and dominating it, rose the long, irregular line of hill-tops of which Castle-an-Dinas is the culminating point.

To Joel Tregurtha, standing smoking at his cottage door of an evening, the huge, peaked hill, with the mouldering ruin on its crest, was a perpetual provocation and challenge to thought. At midsummer the sun set directly behind it, lighting up its shoulders with his enormous rays, and filling the heavens behind it with the largess of his gold: while in winter "the owld haythen," as Joel irreverently termed the sun, setting farther towards the south, glorified certain of the lower hill-tops, leaving the slopes of Castle-an-Dinas weighted with gloom.

To Joel the hill seemed to have a sentient individuality. He could imagine it rejoicing in its glowing crown at mid-summer, and grieving inarticulately when it was lashed and sodden with the rains and the sun bestowed his favours on the rivals at its side.

As a lad, when he had to rise shivering in the mornings, that he might be in time to start work at the mine at seven o'clock, Joel used to glance up at the long dun slopes, which stretched far above the chimneys and buildings of the mine, and occasionally he would mutter, as he ran along the road, "Darn it all! wish I was thee, thee gayte duffer! nawthin' to do all day but set there in the sun."

As he grew older, however, he was less jealous of the hill. He had now a bonny little sweetheart to stare at and wonder over, and no mere lump of granite, though a very god for idleness, could ever taste a pleasure such as sweethearting could supply.

But sweethearting seemed likely to be a rather long affair. One could not get married on ten shillings a week, especially when one had a widowed mother to consider : and in many ways life seemed to become a rather confused tangle. One must wait upon Providence, evidently, and hope for the best.

Through it all, however, the great hill stood there patiently, apparently as stable as the solid earth itself. The gulls winged their way across it and the skylarks mounted above it singing, and the ferns and heather clothed it with their thick green tangles, and it sheltered the fox and the rabbit and the lizard and the snake ; but whether it rejoiced at these things or merely endured them passively, was as much a mystery as the unvoiced secrets of a heart.

And just as sluggishly Joel Tregurtha lived in his groove. Almost as powerless to unclasp the iron hands of Circumstance as was the great green giant that he watched so wistfully, Joel endured his existence patiently and made no complaint.

By-and-by his sweetheart grew weary of waiting for him. She was in the heyday of her life, with her wishes all unrealized, and her day-dreams began to haunt her, moving as shadows among her thoughts.

Joel was by this time a man ; but heavily burdened. His sister, who was always ailing, still lived at home unmarried; and his mother, though she was now an aged woman, was hale and hearty yet and, he hoped, would live for years. He was as weighted with expense as if he were a married man, though the pleasure of possessing a wife was denied to him.

He represented to his sweetheart the position of affairs and begged her to wait for him—something might possibly turn up: though what the "something" was likely to be he neither defined to her nor to himself.

"Why not go to America like the awthers?" asked Lizzie.

Joel looked up at Castle-an-Dinas, now black against the golden after-glow, and a queer feeling of forlornness seemed to clutch him at the heart.

"Iss . . . I cud do that," he muttered, hoarsely.

"If thee'll go to America, I doan't mind waitin' for 'ee," said Lizzie.

"I'll think it ovver," said Joel; and went home greatly perturbed.

All that night Joel tossed sleeplessly on his bed: his love for Lizzie, and his even deeper love for his cradle-land, filling his mind with a turmoil of wishes and regrets that tired him more than a hard day's work.

"Wha's wrong weth 'ee, Joel?" his mother called to him from her bedroom; hearing the sounds of his restless tossings. "Anything the matter weth 'ee? Shall I git up an' maake a cup o' tay? Oppen the winda, ef thee find it too close."

"All right, mawther; 'tes the het, b'leeve," said Joel. "I'll oppen the winda a bit an' go to slaip."

"Iss, do," said Biddy; "else thee'll be fine an' tired tomorra."

So Joel rattled the window noisily, and Biddy went to sleep.

But there was no sleep for Joel for hours yet. Not that he was thinking very clearly or connectedly: he was rather suffering from a sense of unusual bewilderment; a feeling as if he were oppressed by a suffocating weight.

He fell asleep at last through sheer weariness, and did not wake till he heard his mother calling to him from her bed-room: "Jo-el! Jo-el! 'tes time to git up!"

He managed to see Lizzie on the following evening and informed her that he would go to America, as she had suggested.

" When 'ull 'ee start ? " she asked, eagerly.

" In the spring," said Joel.

" O-h ! " said Lizzie. " Tha's anawther sex months."

"It'll taake all that time to get ready," he replied.

"Well," said Lizzie, dubiously, "s'pose we must wait."

All that winter Joel was full of unrest. It was as if some misfortune were stealing on him stealthily and he could faintly hear the approach of his enemy, though unaware of the form in which it would appear. He would stand for an hour at a time smoking at his door, contemplating the long, irregular line of hills with the windy sky stretching greyly behind them and on either hand the steel-blue glint of the sea. For here, on the sloping heights above Goldsithney, one could see across the narrow neck of the pensinsula, and from Joel's little cottage the two channels were visible, with the superb panorama of the rugged hills to boot. And the man's heart yearned towards the familiar

landmarks, as the heart of a mother
towards the faces that have surrounded
her table, and out of whose traits the net
of memory has been spun. The wide
expanse of scenery fronting him daily, if
not an inspiration was, at least, a steady-
ing influence. The love and mercy of
God were more believable to him here
than they would be if he were shut up in
some eye-restricting valley, or, worst of
all, were prisoned helplessly among the
buildings of a town. How could he
leave the hills of his own dear Cornwall?
The distant glimpses of Penzance, St.
Michael's Mount, Castle-an-Dinas—it
would surely break his heart if he had to
give up these! And vague and inarticulate though the sorrow within him was, its
effect grew still more noticeable every day.

"Thee doan't seem happy," said
Lizzie, suspiciously.

"No, nor I arn't," said Joel, lifelessly.

And the pleasures of sweethearting "dragged" in sympathy with the mood.

"Arn't 'ee 'most ready for startin?" asked Lizzie, when the winds of March began to wail across the peninsula and the long brown hill-slopes were beginning to be splashed with green.

"To tell 'ee the truth," said Joel, hesitatingly, "mawther ben beggin' me not to layve her. She's owld; an' she's afeerd she'll never see me no more. I think, b'leeve, I'll ha' to stay home, after all."

"Then it must be all ovver between us," said Lizzie, firmly. "I'm losin' all the fun o' life, hangin' on like this." And he was aware of the angry discontent in her eyes.

He would have pleaded with her, but words always came to him confusedly:

and, in a case like this, the difficulties of expression were insurmountable. He had his feelings—if she would only interpret them as easily as she seemed to interpret his affection if he merely put his lips to hers ! But language he knew well he could not manipulate. If he had to explain his feelings in words, then there was no hope for him.

"O' coorse, ef thee put thy mawther before *me* . . . ." and Lizzie waited to hear a possible disclaimer. "I must look after meself as thee waan't, simminly : it had better be off between us," she added, presently.

"Ef it must be, s'pose it must," said Joel, helplessly.

And with this they parted dumbly in a suddenly-darkened world.

If Joel grieved for the loss of his sweetheart, his grief was inarticulate. He

N

ate his meals as usual, and went to mine as regularly as of old. More than this one could only have affirmed of him by a stretch of imagination, for he made no attempt to discuss the matter, remaining as stolidly incommunicative as a cormorant on a rock.

Lizzie, being a rather attractive young woman, though no longer in the first bloom of girlhood, presently found another sweetheart in the village; and, about twelve months after her parting from Joel, she had the pleasure of standing before the parson as a bride.

Joel made no attempt to find a second sweetheart : he devoted himself, instead, to making his mother comfortable and to living as inoffensively and quietly as his surroundings would permit.

Often, as he stood at the cottage door of an evening, he would fall to musing

over the perplexing puzzle of life, and a
flavour of something like hopelessness
would become perceptible in his thoughts.
But, before he had been long solacing
himself with his pipe, his eyes would
seek, and rest contentedly on, their
familiar landmark, and, therewith, his
sour dissatisfaction would vanish as
rapidly as the flush of a winter sunset,
and an almost bovine quiet would settle
on his thoughts. The great solemn hill,
with its sure foothold in the world and
its simple, primitive wants and pleasures,
affected him as if it were a human
companion : only a companion cleansed
from human passions and infirmities ;
strong, unselfish, perennially calm.

When Lizzie became a mother, Joel
looked at the infant wistfully, and with a
vague twitch of pain in the recesses of his
heart. But as Lizzie herself remained

good-temperedly stolid, without a sign of
unusualness either in her eyes or at her
lips, he ultimately settled down to the
acceptance of her maternity and was as
kind as a godfather to her chubby little
boy.

About ten years after Lizzie's marriage,
when she was a stout and pleasant matron
with a troop of sturdy children, Joel's
mother passed away peacefully and almost
painlessly, and he was left alone with his
sister—now a soured old maid.

Joel still lived in the same thatched
cottage in which he had been born forty
years before, and the rugged granite hill-
tops were still the companions of his
musings as he stood smoking of an evening between the posts of the door.
Through all the changes and crowding
disappointments of his life he had never
wavered in his affection for the great dun

hill, whose crest his eyes sought instinctively morning and night : and its power to soothe him and to attemper his thoughts to patience, seemed, if anything, to have grown with the advancing years. He was as quiet under impositions, and as unresentful of wrongs, as the placid hill that carried its burden of cottages and mine-stacks, as cheerfully as it carried its airy tuft of ferns.

One day Joel's sister took to her bed. According to the doctor, she was suffering from some grave internal ailment and there was little likelihood that she would ever be better while she lived.

This, of course, meant an additional burden for Joel; but he bore it uncomplainingly and with small expenditure of words.

During the long drudgery of his life he had always been careful, and he had managed to save about thirteen pounds. But now this treasured hoard had constantly to be drawn upon, and he saw it gradually melting away before his eyes.

Joel tried to wean himself from his beloved pipe : but this bit of heroism he was unable to accomplish. He, however, reduced his allowance of tobacco from an ounce to less than half an ounce a week, and contented himself, when he was short of the "weed," by merely keeping the empty pipe nursed between his lips.

His sister lingered long enough to practically exhaust his savings, leaving him, at her death, with barely a pound in hand.

He could not make up his mind to have her buried by the parish, so the remainder of his savings he expended on her funeral, and, at forty-five, started the world afresh with nothing but his wages of three pounds a month.

After the death of his sister, Joel lived alone : getting a woman to drop in occasionally to do the chores, but otherwise attending to everything himself.

He felt poor and depressed and very lonely, and, for the first time in his life, thoroughly disheartened with everything. His world seemed empty : and even his pipe had lost its flavour like everything else.

But when he went to the door of his cottage and turned his eyes to the hills, the feeble ticking of self in a great empty world seemed to die away completely : and the mysterious tranquillity of the hills fell on him—the deep, grave calm of the wise and ancient hills.

He stood for hours gazing at the long, green barrier, with the villages at its feet and the sky above its head, and a peculiar exaltation took possession of him. He was glad of the beauty of the world, and he rejoiced, with awe, at its many mysteries. Surely, after all, life was not an empty riddle, though its meaning might wisely be hidden from us here. He watched the sunset almost reverently : the hills were patient, and he could wait.

About eighteen months after Joel's sister died, his old sweetheart, Lizzie, became a widow; her husband having succumbed to an attack of typhoid fever.

Though he was now nearly fifty, Joel had some thoughts of by-and-by asking Lizzie to marry him : and Lizzie, on her part, seemed to be expecting some such offer, if one might judge by the increased friendliness of her attitude towards him.

While matters were in this unsettled state—Joel eyeing Lizzie wistfully, and

Lizzie meeting him more than half-way—
Joel still continued going to mine as
regularly as of old, never missing a
" coor " on any pretence.

One summer evening, when he was
what is called " night coor," Joel, in
passing Lizzie's cottage, saw her standing
at the door, and they exchanged a few
words of halting gossip.

" Thee must find it lonely comin' home
of a mornin'," said Lizzie, " not a bit o'
fire in the house, an' nowan to give 'ee a
cup o' tay. I'll give 'ee a kittle of hot
water when thee'rt passin' tomorra, ef
thee like."

" Thaank 'ee," said Joel, awkwardly. " I
shall be glad to have un, you."

" Tap to the door in passin', an' I'll
have un ready for 'ee."

" Thaank 'ee, I will : an' much obliged
to 'ee," said Joel.

And they parted with a nod and a
friendly "good-night."

The next morning Lizzie was up before
five—though she knew Joel could not call
for the water till nearly seven—and by six
o'clock she had the kettle ready on the
hob and was warming a huge pasty in the
oven as an additional peace-offering for
her old sweetheart.

Suddenly a lad, with a white scared face,
came clattering up the empty roadway.

" Heerd the news ? " he called out, as
she came to the door on hearing the foot-
steps.

" No ! what news? Anything happened
down to mine ? "

" Bra' bad accident in shuttin'* wan o'
the hawls ! Wan man killed, an' two or
three hurt ! "

" Do 'ee knaw their names ? " asked

* Shooting = blasting.

Lizzie, suddenly paling with apprehen-
sion.

"Joel Tregurtha es killed, an' Dicky
Fire have lost 'es haand, an' owld Bob
Hurry's skat blind!" said the lad.

Lizzie went indoors and seated herself
heavily on a chair.

She sat there for quite a considerable
time ; her hands on her lap, and her eyes
wandering vaguely around the homely
little room.

Presently she was aware of the smell of
something burning. It was the pasty beginning to blacken in the oven.

She jumped up hastily. "It'll do for
the children," she ejaculated.

And just then there was the sound of
trampling feet in the roadway.

She placed the pasty on a plate and
rushed to the door.

Past the little chapel came a group

of miners with a litter, over which two of them had considerately placed their coats.

"Who es 'a?" she asked, staring at the litter on their shoulders.

"Joel Tregurtha, poor fella!" said one of the bearers. "He was killed in shuttin' a hawl laast night."

"Poor fella!" said Lizzie. And again: "Poor fella!"

"Good job 'a got nowan to layve behind un," said the bearer.

"Poor fella!" said Lizzie: and went indoors.

THE GIFTS OF THE LITTLE GREY MAN.

THE GIFTS OF THE LITTLE GREY MAN.

In one of the most crowded of the metropolitan thoroughfares, in the busiest part of the afternoon, a little grey man, of abnormal leanness, stood hawking some tiny cubes of crystal.

He carried a small mahogany tray, which was supported against his chest by a stout leather strap, and on this highly-polished tray—it had a surface like a mirror—the tiny cubes lay scattered carelessly.

Instead of advertising his wares with blatant importunity, the hawker had a

card nailed conspicuously on the tray,
with these words neatly written on it :—

YOU ARE WELCOME TO THE GIFTS OF
THE LITTLE GREY MAN.

The only thing he did to attract
attention was play on a long, old-
fashioned fiddle. From this he evoked
such odd, suggestive melodies—not so
much sweet or beautiful fancies as
fascinating caprices with the most
outrè effects—that when, through the
fluctuating din of the traffic, the weird
notes travelled to the ears of a passer-by,
they seemed to vibrate in the deepest
chords of his nature and set free thoughts
as primal as his blood.

As often as not, the passer-by would
rush past the musician, eyeing him
askance with a kind of terrified scrutiny ;
a nameless trouble throbbing furtively in

his heart. 'Who is this man, that he can touch the springs of memory thus subtly? Does he know, or merely surmise? I have not been thinking aloud, surely!' And the wayfarer would hurry on troubled and perplexed.

Occasionally, however, one would turn to glance at the tray, and, after reading the card, would shake his head and pass on. To these men of the city who saw everything bought and sold—a pair of gloves or a horse, a man or a woman, all of them purchasable—the idea of a gift seemed a mockery and an absurdity. They were too old now to be taken in by such a trick. But though they passed on mentally pluming themselves on their shrewdness, they kept musing on the oddity of the offer none the less.

Finally one of them turned back and took up a crystal from the tray.

"What's the trick?" asked he, with assumed indifference.

The little grey man made no reply. But so penetratingly subtle were the strains of the fiddle, or such magic was gathered within the simple weft of sounds, that it seemed to the man, as he stood gazing at the crystal, that he could hear a dialogue proceeding somewhere in the remote distance: a dialogue that apparently directly concerned himself.

'*Do you call that ragged life a success?*'

'*I gave him everything that might enable him to make it such.*'

'*But is it a success?*'

'*What leads you to think it otherwise?*'

'*What a wonderful soul you gave him: it was a masterpiece, was it not? Infinite*

*in its range of qualities and in its subtle
adaptabilities, it was to be as flawless as a
diamond, and as indestructible as . . . .
yourself!* But the atmosphere in which
*it has been compelled to exert itself has
apparently told cruelly on its qualities and
its texture. The breath of its fellow-men,
the atmosphere of its surroundings, these
have corroded it strangely and fatally, it
seems to me. Look down through his eyes
into the unclean depths of him: is that
ragged and rotten soul the masterpiece you
were so proud of? Would it not have
been wisest to have left out that bit of
mechanism, or, at any rate, to have
curtailed its capacity for self-destruction?'*
and a burst of sneering laughter seemed
to echo along the strings.

So poignantly suggestive was the
sudden drift of thoughts, that the man
who held the crystal knew himself only

by his memories, and the flavour of these seemed bitter beyond belief.

" It is all right, then ? Can I take it ? " questioned the man.

The peddler kept on working his bow.

The man nodded gravely. " Thank you ; I think I shall appreciate it," said he.   And with that he walked away with the crystal in his hand.

'REST IN ANY FORM YOU WISH : BUT A SINGLE WISH ONLY.'

Such was the legend graved deeply on the crystal : and the man had made his choice and was ready with his wish.

" I should like to pass the remainder of my life untortured by desire," he mused, as he sat that evening at his wine.

And the wish began at once to be subtly fulfilled.

The book he had been glancing at he

no longer desired to read. He leaned back and closed his eyes and presently he was asleep.

And from that day onward desire died out of him.

He neither cared to gaze on nature, nor to lounge at the theatre : and business and its cares were simply detestable to him. Probably he had energy latent somewhere in his nature, but it never came to the front or availed him in any way. The bias towards restfulness was so pronounced and irresistible that he sank into slothfulness as one sinks into a slough.

His business went to ruin; and his life went to ruin with it. But he was persistently and irritatingly content through it all.

The lives that depended on him found their support a rotten one and dropped off dejectedly into the black abysses of the world : but even when he came to die he was smilingly contented.

He had craved that desire might be permanently rooted out of him; and whether it were a wise or foolish one, the wish had been fulfilled.

PASSING ON.

PASSING ON.

I.

THE hired nurse came to the bedside and bent over me carelessly.

" He will soon pass now," she muttered, as if relieved. "Perhaps if I open the window it will make him pass easier." And with that she went to the window and opened it widely to the night.

A lean face stared in out of the darkness : a face with cavernous eyes, fixed and lidless, and with a brow as dry and fleshless as a bleached white bone.

The eyes seemed to hold me, to draw me towards them irresistibly. It was as if

something wavered, dissolved, sank helplessly within me : as if stupefying vapours
rolled duskily across my eyeballs ; as if my
blood thickened dully . . . . and my life
died out.

And then came a sudden unaccountable buoyancy. I looked down on the
rigid countenance lying helpless among
the pillows; on the rigid form outlined
beneath the thin, white counterpane. I
could have pitied the figure, so forlorn and
useless—such a mere blank wreck, cast
aside and abandoned—but the Face
within the darkness seemed to compel me
towards it, and suddenly I was outside
with it in the dense black night, and the
Form the face belonged to held me
gathered to its side.

I turned once, and only once, looking
over its shoulder, to cast a glance at the
tiny square of light we were leaving : the

window of the room in which I had lived
and had died. Then the night closed
round me with its shroud of darkness, and
I could hear the far sea rolling and moaning beneath my feet.

II.

I was abandoned even by the Form
that had borne me hither. As the darkness slid away in misty folds, I was conscious of a world broadening remorselessly
around me, and was aware that I stood in
the Undiscovered Land.

There was, apparently, no hiatus in life,
after all. The mere material background
had changed its character and its appeal
—there were neither house nor shops, nor
the seductions of commerce or of things
conventional—but the passions and
desires, the wishes and cravings of the

human consciousness were by no means dead or eradicated even here.

I saw a man I had met somewhere in that past life of mine and whom I remembered as being considered impregnably virtuous. He was religious, of course; dabbled in generous actions as a pastime; was a Sunday-school teacher; and occasionally used to preach. I saw him here dogged with a most repulsive shadow that evidently caused the good man the most exquisite annoyance. When he passed a young girl, or even a flourishing matron, his shadow took the semblance of a hungry satyr, brimming over with appetite and unrestrained in desire. If he passed a godly fellow-worker, or a man rich or merely respectable, his shadow had an apish, leering enviousness and a suggestion of almost impish malevolence. It was painfully annoying, this rude travesty of his emotions—which, of course, were unaffectedly pious and modest—and to a man so exquisitely constituted the torture must have been great. I pitied him heartily: and yet I could scarcely repress a smile.

There was a man who on earth had been a noted philanthropist, with a heart big enough to embrace in it all the suffering ones of earth. Here his heart was so small and dry and withered, that, as he walked to and fro, it hopped up and down in his bosom like a parched bean shaken up and down in a pail.

There was another gaunt stranger pacing to and fro along the highway who on earth had passed for one of the most unselfish of men. They had his statue in the market-place and his model lodging-houses in the slums. Here he was nothing but the mere bony skeleton of his

self-hood—the ego warped and very rotten
and as naked as a bone. It was amusing
to see how persistently the poor wretch
kept plucking handfuls of grass and scrap-
ing up the leaves that strewed the roadside
that he might weave out of these a garment
to hide his nakedness : and then, *puff!* a
breath of wind—and he was appallingly
nude again.

In an iron cage there was a strange
collection of curiosities, which a sleepy
old greybeard pointed out between his
dozes : beginning an eulogy, then dropping
asleep in the middle of it, and waking up
to end the description by a jest. He had
a man who had written books—sacrificing
everything to the writing of them—and
here was the poor creature now with a
mass of manuscript for a heart and with
rillets of ink trickling feebly through his
veins. He had an " honourable and

gallant " soldier, so arrant a coward that, being shut up in a compartment with a frisky little spectre, he was continually imploring someone to burst in and protect him : even entreating a woman, whom he had ruined and flung aside, that she would come and share his misery and shield his body with her own. He had an endless variety of oddities, this sleepy old greybeard, but his eulogies and his satire were so inextricably tangled that it was a weariness to listen to him and I was glad to pass on.

But this passing on was, after all, a process interminable. The land was fuller of marvels than an ant-hill is of ants : and the tragedies, the oddities, the grotesquerie of its revelations, make my sides ache with laughter . . . . for I am passing on still.

Woodfall & Kinder, Printers, 70–76, Long Acre, W.C.

By the same Author.

DROLLS FROM SHADOWLAND.

(Uniform with TALES OF THE MASQUE.)

One Vol.   18mo, 3s. 6d.

" They are so simple at first sight that one is surprised by their depth of suggestion, which satisfies Milton's definition of the old tales of enchantment, 'where more is meant than meets the ear.' . . . . There is genius of an uncommon kind in these 'Drolls from Shadowland.' "— R. H. STODDARD, in the *Mail and Express* (New York).

" They are all clever and powerful, highly imaginative and weirdly fantastic.   The tales are full of character and excellent of their kind."— —*Guardian.*

" Beautiful to read from their deep imagination and haunting in their allegorical depth.   Mournful, but not bitter ; brief, but not slight ; subtle, but not obscure, in their hidden meanings, these 'Drolls from Shadowland' suggest nothing in English literature.   Their art is as consummate as Daudet's.   This is a masterpiece."—*Traveller* (Boston, U.S.A.).

" This is a book in which poetry and prose are blent.   Mr. Pearce suggests subtly and never insists. His is imagination of a fine kind, and one feels confident that this little book will give him an assured place."—*Illustrated London News*.

"All are marked by graceful fancy and imaginative power."—*Speaker*.

"Mr. Pearce has a weird imagination and an unusual gift of curdling the blood with a few strokes of the pen."—*Academy*.

"They are full of human interest, and though a pungent but not unkindly satire gives them tone and quality, the satire is tempered with a broad and generous sympathy. Each of these sketches has some core of truth expressed with great beauty."—*Bradford Observer*.

"The enormous truths of life wink at us mysteriously out of dainty, elusive, fluttering, glinting pictures."—*Pall Mall Gazette*.

"This most notable work."—*Boston Advertiser* (U.S.A.).

By W. B. YEATS.

THE CELTIC TWILIGHT.

Men and Women, Dhouls and Faeries.

One Vol. 18mo, 3s. 6d.

"For a pleasant, pathetic, charming view of Irish people and Irish manners, no modern writer is to be matched with Mr. Yeats."—ANDREW LANG, in the *Illustrated London News*.

"Mr. Yeats has dwelled in the dim kingdom of dhouls and fairies, of ghosts and witches, and lived among those who still hold commerce with the good people, and tell strange stories of the haunted glens and waterways of the green hills of Ireland."—*Saturday Review.*

"This book, which begins and ends with a strain of exquisite music in verse, is written for the most part in prose which is lyrical in feeling, though restrained always within the most modest limits of prose rhythms. It is such stuff as dreams are made of, admitting us for a moment to see 'how man mounts to the infinite by the ladder of the impossible.' And so it has a charm and value beyond its actual merit as a piece of writing; it opens up new horizons, too often obscured for us by the smoke and chimney pots of cities; it reasserts the eternal reality of romance."—*Athenæum.*

"It belongs to the shy and quiet things of literature. It is all in twilight tones, and you need to be used to walking in a grey dim light before you recognize its beauty."—*Sketch.*

"Legends and dreams and fancies succeed each other in a veritable phantasmagoria in Mr. Yeats's remarkable book, to which we would gladly devote more space, but that we could hardly give a fair idea of it without quoting it in its entirety."—*Spectator.*

By **KATHARINE TYNAN** (Mrs. Hinkson).

A CLUSTER OF NUTS,

Being Sketches among my Own People.

" Kindly Irish of the Irish,
Neither Saxon nor Italian."

Crown 8vo, 3s. 6d.

"Charming, tender, haunting—these are the words that best describe one's impressions of Mrs. Hinkson's 'Cluster of Nuts.' . . . There is no plot in any of the stories, but each is a graceful and tender outline of some phase of Irish character."—*Academy.*

"It amazes you as much as it touches you to find the scenes and sorrows of a peasant's set-grey life made as picturesque, lovely, and moving as a sombre moor is made by the glow of the sunset."—*Truth.*

"The book is admirable reading, tender, re-strained, and winning."—*National Observer.*

"Vaguely sad, pleasantly pathetic are the stories that might have been deeply tragic seen from another point of view, and for this reason we prefer those that are memories of childhood, for the standpoint of Mrs. Hinkson is the standpoint of every natural, healthy, dreamy child. The cup-moss, the fairy rings, the tame pigeon, and the apple-trees are life's realities, and the love tragedies of the grown-up folk are as the Greek mythology will be in twenty years to come : she is never too much absorbed in them to refrain from the playful yet wistful digressions that make up so much of the charm of this ' Cluster of Nuts.'"—*Athenæum.*

By MAURUS JÓKAI.

EYES LIKE THE SEA.

A ROMANCE.

Translated from the Hungarian of MAURUS JÓKAI by R. NISBET BAIN.

One Vol. Crown 8vo, 6s.

" In some respects the heroine reminds us of Becky Sharp, and in others of Manon Lescaut, and in feminine dexterity and sexual eccentricities is no unworthy mate for either."—*Athenæum.*

"The vigour of the book is astonishing."
—*World.*

" 'Eyes like the Sea' is one of those rare books that break all the rules and defy criticism by justifying their irregularities."—*Guardian.*

"The great charm of the book is the manner in which Jókai analyses Bessy's character. All through the story, indeed, we feel ourselves in the presence of a master of the human heart, and again and again we come upon sentences pregnant with that wisdom which it is the lot of but few to acquire."—*Speaker*.

By MOIRA O'NEILL.

AN EASTER VACATION.

A NOVEL.

One Vol. Crown 8vo.

"One of those clever books which do not irritate by an aggressive display of cleverness, but please in a quiet way by being always simply right."—*Academy*.

"Man, from woman's point of view, is treated with quiet sagacity and humour. Her people are well-mannered and amusing folk, who live and move and have their being in ease and comfort."—*Athenæum*.

"It gives pleasant hopes of future good work."—*Guardian*.

"The reader may pick by the dozen out of the pages shrewd, witty, pungent, thoughtful remarks, humorous comparisons, bits of satire, sly and compact, and we confidently bid him go and do it."—*World*.

Mr. GEORGE GISSING'S NOVELS.

Denzil Quarrier. *One Vol. Crown 8vo, 6s.*

The Emancipated. *One Vol. Crown 8vo, 6s.*

The Odd Women. *One Vol. Crown 8vo, 6s.*

"A little buoyancy, a little of the joy of earth, of the spirit of Mr. Meredith—nay, or of Rabelais—what is the use of wishing these things to a talent radically different? It is much if such a talent can end as Mr. Gissing's seems likely to, in a creed that is somewhat dreary, but still strenuous, self-contained, and not desperate nor without dignity."—*Manchester Guardian.*

"Certainly his people live. You might brush against many of them in the Strand from morning till morning again. And, better, they live transfigured by the artist, who shews you the exact significance of each life. 'The Odd Women' is a great vindication of realism from the charge of dulness."—*Pall Mall Gazette.*

"Mr. Gissing's new novel 'The Odd Women' is intensely modern, actual in theme as well as in treatment. . . . The book is better than merely readable, it is absorbing. One feels that the author is more than master of his subject; that he has turned it about and around, and thoroughly knows its capabilities."—*Athenæum.*